A QUIET MURDER

A JOSH SUTTON MYSTERY

D.B. CRAWFORD

Description: First U.S. edition. First International edition.

Identifiers: Library of Congress Control Number 2021913566

ISBN: 978-1-7776274-3-0

Ebook ISBN: 978-1-7776274-4-7

Subjects: Sutton, Josh (fictitious character) – Fiction

GSAFD: Crime suspense fiction

BISAC: FICTION/crime/police/pandemic

First U.S. Edition: October 2021

First International Edition October 2021

DBC

For Mackenzie, Scott and Jackson

CHAPTER ONE

Whenever his division in the northwest section of Toronto was enjoying a lull in its workload major crime detective Josh Sutton found some release in driving his sedan for an after-lunch inspection of the upper stretch of Marshall Road. After making medical grade masks instead of bed linens during the pandemic, the Marshall factory, the only structure on the road, was temporarily closed. The owners were seizing the opportunity to upgrade their installation because business was still somewhat stuttering on its way to the level enjoyed before the pandemic. There was a posted sign at the corner warning against parking on that dead end section, but people up to no good paid it no mind.

He turned the corner and, as usual, parked his car some distance in, let the window down then yelled: "Fucking virus, fucking pandemic" several times. It helped him, and his therapist approved of the bizarre therapeutic effort. Whatever worked was her motto when helping those who grieved because everyone did it differently, each on their own secret schedule.

On their regular sessions she made a point of telling Sutton that the pain would eventually lessen. He did not believe her. Not yet anyway. It was still too deep.

After a few minutes, he felt that he had marginally reduced the invisible grip of the sorrow still clinging to his heart. With the window still down, Josh breathed deeply a few times, something he made a point of doing every day. As his therapist reminded him often, he had to concentrate on the good things in his life.

And spring was one of them.

Actually, spring was Josh Sutton's favourite time of year. The newness of it all made him hope that this year the tide would ebb toward a more satisfying vitality. And today was especially agreeable as the sun shone high in the clear blue sky. Even if the temperatures were still on the cool side, the promise of a warming trend made him smile while hoping the rains of April would soon complete their duty of helping May flowers flourish.

He started his vehicle, very cognisant that the potholes resulting from the many trucks travelling on the road's surface demanded particular attention from drivers at this time of year. He did not see any parked cars, but he knew that that could change once he made the curve ahead. He had caught many people in that last section of the road over the winter. There had been many dealers meeting suppliers for a quick deal, but the strangest, and most interesting in a way he supposed, was the middle-aged couple he came upon who were in a rather compromising situation.

Josh had parked his sedan behind the black SUV to walk over and investigate. He quickly realized that it was a good thing the motor was running and that a bit of the driver's side window was down to keep the pair safe and warm in January as they enjoyed each other's mostly naked bodies on the pulled down back seat. For a moment, he was unsure what he should do. He figured both were married colleagues who could only enjoy a tryst during their lunch break. In all probability they both worked for one of the large companies with operations on the lower section of Marshall Road.

He knocked softly on the window, and the woman's face appeared above the man's shoulders. "What do you want? We're adults, we can do whatever we want," she said.

Josh reminded them that they should abide by the sign that parking was not permitted on that section of the road, and added: "I would think a motel would be a lot more comfortable. Get going. I'll be checking back soon," he admonished as he walked back toward his ride.

He had gone to turn around at the entrance to the Marshall factory and, thankfully, when he continued back down the SUV had disappeared, otherwise he probably would not have known what to do. He didn't think he could charge them with anything. After all, while it was naughty and immoral, adultery, which he figured that was, was not a crime in the usual sense. Remembering the incident always made him smile. In its own way, it had been a good thing because it had taken his mind off his reality.

For a while at least.

Now, on taking the curve of the road, Josh saw a white sedan, late model he judged, parked on the other side of the road. He was sure he saw someone's head on the steering wheel. Murder immediately came to mind. While investigating homicides was his main duty, he considered murders to be not only painful but dangerous all around. He continued driving slowly and pressed the button to bring his window down again while he stopped close to the sedan. The driver's side window was also down and he saw a woman loudly wailing as she seemingly used the steering wheel as a support for her head.

Josh had seen many women cry during the course of his more than fifteen years in law enforcement, but none as loud and desperate as this one. He drove on until he could turn around and come to a stop just behind the sedan. When he got out, the loudness of the weeping had not subsided. He slowly walked to the open window.

"Ma'am, do you need help?" She didn't seem to hear as the crying continued. "Are you having car problems? Do you want me to call someone for you?"

Sutton was wondering how he could help during the several minutes that passed before the crying began to lessen and she lifted her head off the steering wheel. Without looking at Josh, she reached for tissues from the box on the passenger seat and loudly blew her nose.

Josh repeated his offer. "Do you want me to call someone for you?"

Still not looking at him, she shook her head.

"I can't just leave you here like this. Are you hurt? Did something happen?"

The residue of the crying made her shoulders bob up and down as she finally looked at Josh and said: "I just needed to cry."

"May I ask why?"

"My husband died yesterday," she replied as she again blew her nose and pulled down the rear view mirror so she could contour her eyes with a tissue. "I just needed to cry."

Josh was totally at a loss for words. From time to time he had to inform family members of the death of a loved one but that was quite different from what was in front of him now. He had mastered comforting words for those who stayed behind, but the woman in front of him had him baffled. She was an attractive redhead in her late forties, he guessed. It surprised him that her eyes were very dark. "You have my sympathy. May I ask what happened?"

After a moment she said simply: "Heart attack."

She wiped her nose once more, sighed loudly then pressed the starter button. Slowly she drove forward getting back on the road while sending Josh a somewhat hesitant wave.

Josh looked at the car for a while as it drove away before getting back into his own car. He could not shake the feeling that things were not as they appeared. His instincts told him that something else beside the husband's death was at work here.

He always trusted his instincts.

Back at his desk in the division office, Josh was keying in the numbers and letters of the license plate of the white sedan into his computer when his junior colleague came in. Ross Walters was tall with skin the colour of warm mahogany along with a well-shaped shaved head. Sutton never understood his colleague's explanation that he was going bald so why not shave it all. Sutton suspected that bachelor Walters thought women found his look sexy.

"So, find any naked bodies on your exploration today?" Walters asked.

Josh grinned briefly. "Not quite. What I did find was a woman crying ... what am I saying? I never heard such loud wailing. It was almost as if a bunch of people were sobbing at the same time. She said her husband had just died. I'm running her plate. Here we are: Brenda Castle." He searched deeper. "Married to one Murray Castle."

"Murray Castle? The lawyer? A buddy of mine hired him a few years back and was very satisfied. There was an article about his firm in *The Star* a couple of months back."

"What kind of lawyer?"

"Strictly business matters if I remember correctly."

"There she is," Josh said. "The crying lady is Dr. Brenda Castle, a psychologist."

"No wonder she was crying," Walters commented. "According to the article Murray was being sued by a client for having lost him money in some deal or other. For millions. I would cry too if I were in her shoes."

"Was it settled?"

"Don't know. Didn't follow up."

Josh found the newspaper article online and began reading all about the firm of Mercer Davis Carroll and Castle.

CHAPTER TWO

Brenda Castle was very tired. It was as if crying for a long time in her car had depleted all her energy. Her caring mother was, again, at her house trying to help but she only got on Brenda's nerves.

"Mother, why don't you go home and rest," she said softly.

Fully aware that Brenda said mother instead of mom when she was annoyed, the older woman defended herself. "I just want to help you. To see you through this."

"I know, but you've done enough. Perhaps you could go bake some sweets for after the funeral."

"Great idea. Are you going to be okay?"

"Of course. Sally will be home soon. Don't worry," Brenda said, gently guiding her mother toward the front door. Once the door closed Brenda let out a long sigh of relief. She had to figure out what she was going to do, and how, and her mother was certainly not the right person to ask for advice. As far as Brenda knew her mother was not aware of the legal trouble Murray had gotten into. At least she hoped.

Brenda was facing many challenges. The first one was to arrange the funeral as soon as possible to spare her two children any further pain if at all possible. The realization that their father had died suddenly had been a blow to both her son, Malcolm, who had recently joined his dad's firm as a rookie associate, and was with him when he died, and her daughter, Sally, a psychology student who wanted to be as successful and well liked as her mother.

After Murray's client decided to sue him, Brenda wondered how Malcolm could continue to work in the same office, but her son kept saying that he was going to prove his father had acted in his client's best interest. Brenda had her doubts. After all, just like her husband's explanations, her son's arguments seemed lame to her.

Of course she wasn't a lawyer.

Now she felt too tired to examine the issue. She went looking for a movie on television and found a classic comedy which was sure to help her relax and forget. However, after a moment, she muted the sound as thoughts of Murray came to the surface as had often been the case since she had learned that he would no longer be part of her life.

No matter the mistakes he may or may not have made she would always have stood by him. He was a great husband and they had almost never argued. It was as if their thoughts and decisions automatically matched. She knew she was not done crying because she had to release all the shock and the pain she now felt and that would stay with her for years to come, possibly forever.

And, as a father, Murray Castle had been a model for other dads. He had been attentive to his children from day one despite his busy work schedule. She knew that her friends wished their husbands would do the same from time to time.

The tears came and she let them flow.

She wondered once more for the hundredth time if she had been instrumental in his death. Because of her work, of the people she chose to help, Murray had been pressured in a way that could have affected his health. But if she were truly honest she had to admit that that seemed almost impossible because he was in excellent shape physically and otherwise. The pressure Murray faced because of her work would surely not have caused heart failure. He dealt with pressure every day, but he had long ago learned to manage it effectively. So surely the additional pressure could not be construed as being causative.

The movie was ending and Brenda blew her nose one more time. She turned off the television. She had to get some sleep.

Sleeping brought relief from reality, but she was still having trouble getting non interrupted shut-eye which had begun to appear with Murray's legal problems and had continued until his recent amazing request. She was perfectly aware that it would not change her decision as far as the circumstances were concerned, but her mind was still trying to understand how people of means could think that psychological evaluations could be manipulated.

However with Murray now gone she knew she was ready to counteract the request. But not today. At this moment she needed some shut-eye. She reached for the sleeping pill bottle on the nightstand and took one. *No. Make that two,* she mused. *No,* she corrected. *No point in getting addicted.*

Night was not the time for intense thinking although, as she waited for the pill to do its job, she could not avoid recalling how startled she had been at seeing the classically attractive man at the window of her car when her tears had been finally spent. Thankfully, the tall clean-shaven man with kind eyes had just been a caring soul bent on helping her, not a depraved pervert preying on strangers.

In a moment, she was asleep.

Sally Castle was staring at her mother. "Mom, are you okay?"

Brenda opened her eyes, but it took a moment for her to realize that she was in the guest bedroom, and that her daughter was looking at her.

"What's the matter, Sally? I thought you were staying at your friend's place. Why are you here?" she asked, her words slurry.

"You didn't answer your phone."

"So?" Brenda asked. "I turned off my phone so I could sleep without interruptions. You shouldn't worry about me. I slept in because it was late when I finally fell asleep."

"Maybe I can help you with things."

"Sweet of you to offer, but I have nowhere to be. I can't even plan the funeral until your dad's body is released."

"He died of a heart attack. What's the problem?"

"Not sure. Something about the need for an autopsy because according to his medical records he was in perfect health. I don't know what to tell you."

"Weird."

The ringing of the land line phone put a stop to the conversation as Sally went to pick up the instrument on a table on the hallway. A few seconds later she was back. "Mom, it's for you," and handed the receiver to her mother.

After identifying herself, Brenda heard the male voice at the other end of the line say: "The autopsy on your husband has been completed. You can make arrangements to have his body picked up."

"Surely you didn't find anything suspicious."

Brenda heard: "I'm afraid I can't comment on that." Then the line went dead.

She became quickly concerned. What, if anything, had they found? She decided then and there to wait for the official report before reaching any conclusion.

She told Sally that she had to get going to make funeral arrangements.

As she drove to the mortuary, Brenda wondered what exactly the autopsy had revealed, if anything, and questioned why she had not been given the results yet. She was well aware that there were many types of undetectable poisons that could bring on a heart attack but who could have wanted Murray dead? Surely the warnings tossed at Murray could not have resulted in murder. The reasons were not there. She had to stop thinking that they could be the cause of Murray's death because surely that would be insane, yet murder was insanity, was it not?

She knew her husband had not always been the most honest lawyer on the face of the earth. He had boasted to her once that he sometimes looked for ways to pad his charges to clients. When she attempted to make him see that his shenanigans could eventually affect his children, he had simply pointed out that rich people did not know the difference. They didn't check charges on invoices like middle-class people did. They simply paid his bill without questioning anything.

As she pulled her white sedan into a parking space in front of the funeral home, she admonished herself. She had to be strong and wait for confirmation of the cause of death before coming to a conclusion of murder.

A minute later, her son Malcolm pulled in beside her. Another reason to be strong.

CHAPTER THREE

It was now over a year since the pandemic had held Toronto, the country and the world hostage as it killed indiscriminately, and the city was now enjoying a drought in the number of crimes of all sorts. The city law enforcement personnel knew that crimes had remained low since the virus had been conquered and the pandemic stopped in its track. The city was supposed to have returned to normal, but Josh wondered if it ever would. Today's normal was a lot different from the normal of the past. It was as if people had remained afraid to be close to each other, that they had learned to be loners. Like him.

From their informants, the police knew that criminals had been affected because they had heard all the horror stories of the lethal virus being markedly brutal in the number of deaths in the correctional system population. While fully aware that there was always a chance they could be caught and arrested, criminals banked on the fact that they could look forward to getting out of prison if found guilty. Even if the virus had been mostly eradicated in society, getting sick behind bars was still a distinct possibility that they weren't yet ready to chance.

A very efficient vaccination solution had brought life back to the world, but psyches had been damaged. The pain and suffering shown on screens of all sizes for months and months had made tons of victims, not only those that needed traditional health care, but also those that needed reassurance, love and hope.

As he did.

The long-term goal of society in the post-pandemic era, if there ever was one, was to help those poor souls. Sutton was convinced that would-be criminals had been affected like everyone else. He was certain that they were simply extending the pause of their activities and would soon return in full force. Their current idle period was an ideal time for them to elaborate detailed agendas that might require closer attention from law officers once these were put into place.

But the lull was very welcome by the detective. It would give him a chance to spend most of his time on the Murray Castle murder case. His captain had informed him that the lawyer had definitely been the victim of foul play the previous day. An autopsy had been requested by Castle's own physician who had been summoned by Malcolm Castle after his father collapsed in the law office in mid-afternoon. Malcolm had attempted mouth-to-mouth with no success while someone called Dr. Hewell whose office was on the lower floor in the same building.

Dr. Hewell, a physician with more than three decades of experience, had been Murray Castle's doctor for almost twenty years. He knew his patient very well and had no doubt that a heart attack was not only improbable but totally ridiculous. After pronouncing Murray dead, the doctor took time to examine the body and saw signs that required investigation. That's what he was telling Josh Sutton as the two men talked in the physician's office. Sutton had called the doctor immediately upon receiving the autopsy report.

"Can you be more specific as to the signs that didn't sit right with those of a heart attack?"

"I'm hardly an expert on toxins, but I remember enough from my training and from my reading of medical journals that I can detect evidence of poison in a patient. I found Murray's colouring to be off ... I mean off for someone with cardiac problems. And I was certain his legs had been affected which clearly meant a poison.

"Murray was a health nut, to the point of obsession. At his request, I ordered a full battery of cardiac tests a few months ago. Just before Christmas. The results couldn't have been better. Murray exercised every day, ate well, drank little, took vitamins and so forth. He was not a candidate for cardiac problems. That's the reason I ordered an autopsy. I wanted to know the exact cause of death."

"Mr. Castle ingested aconite. You are familiar with it?"

"It's a type of neurotoxin derived from a plant called monkshood. You have quite a job in front of you, detective. Monkshood is not a common flower although it's been seen around here."

"I am well aware of that fact. That's why I'm paid the so-so bucks."

The physician chuckled briefly. "Of course, I suppose only an expert could prepare it for consumption. If you want to contact a person who knows a lot about toxins, may I suggest you contact this gentleman," Hewell said as he wrote a name and number on a piece of paper which he handed to the detective. "He'll be able to answer all your questions about poisons."

"Thank you," Sutton said as he put the paper in his pocket.

"I'm the one who must thank you, detective. Knowing that I made the right decision and that the poison was identified will help me make peace with Murray's passing."

The doctor then added: "I liked Murray. He was very personable."

"Did he talk to you about any duplicity or problems at work?"

"Detective, Murray seldom talked about his work."

"Since you knew him well, did he ever confide in you that he had received threats or anything of that nature?"

"Never said anything along those lines, I assure you."

"Can you tell me if he was happy in his marriage?"

"I know he was. I met Brenda, his wife, once. They seemed to both fit well together."After thanking the doctor, the detective left while wondering if any of what he had learned would be of help as the investigation progressed.

Sutton did not leave the building, one of two identical fifteen-story structures just north of the 401 which crossed the city east to west. The tenants of the buildings, businesses of all types which included health care professionals, catered to Torontonians who did not especially relish the idea of traveling in heavy traffic into the heart of the city.

Sutton made his way to the elevator and pressed the button for the seventh floor where the offices of Mercer Davis Carroll and Castle, barristers and solicitors, were located. Stepping inside he was immediately aware of the heavy presence of money. The lighting was subdued and there was a thick maroon carpet with large swatches of beige covering the floor while the art on the walls was judged by Sutton as being something you'd see in an art gallery or museum. It pointed to the fact that the pandemic had not reduced the standard of law practitioners.

The young attractive receptionist that Sutton estimated was part of the welcoming first impression was seated behind a large desk with modern lines.

The woman smiled warmly at him. How could she help.

He showed her his badge and asked for Gabriel Mercer.

"I'm sorry, but Mr. Mercer is out of town. Until tomorrow. Can someone else help you?"

"How about Malcolm Castle? Is he in?"

"Sorry. His father passed away and he's away for a few days."

"Of course. May I ask if you make the coffee here for the lawyers?"

"I do, yes. Why do you ask? Do you want some?"

"No, thanks, but do you know if Mr. Castle drank coffee in the office here or if he or his assistant bought coffee from outside in paper cups?"

She looked puzzled. "To tell you the truth, I really don't know. I don't think I've ever noticed."

With an understanding nod, Josh asked to see Castle's assistant.

"I'm sorry, but Cecilia is not in. She took a compassionate break because of the death of her boss."

He thanked the young woman, telling her he would be back.

CHAPTER FOUR

As he drove north to Brenda Castle's home, Josh tried to elaborate the type of questions he should ask a lady in her fragile condition. And if her children were with her, did they know the details of their father's life? He decided that, as always, he would let his instincts and logic guide him to the proper line of questioning.

The house stood on a standard piece of land in a subdivision of large homes built perhaps a decade earlier, as far as Sutton remembered, on land vacated when an ancient factory spread out over several acres was finally levelled after years of being abandoned.

The yard in front of the rich beige bricks of the Castle home was being worked on by a gardener with what Sutton thought was an odd-looking rake. Near the house, a few green shoots were beginning to rise in an ode to spring. The white sedan was parked near the front door and there was a red sports car parked in front of the two-car garage next to a classic VW bug. Just like Murray Castle's office, his home flaunted money even before one stepped inside.

He parked near the white sedan and made his way up the three steps to the front door. A young woman, who had surely been crying judging from her red eyes, answered the bell.

"Good afternoon," he said, as he showed his badge. "I'd like to see Mrs. Castle."

The young woman seemed unable to move for a moment as she

eyed the detective. "What is it about? She's not up to seeing anyone right now."

"Perhaps, but it is very important."

"Just a moment," Sally said after a short hesitation, shutting the door on Sutton.

Several minutes passed before the door was again opened. This time Brenda herself, wearing a classic black suit which highlighted her good figure, faced the detective. "Oh!" she exclaimed. "You're the man who saw me cry yesterday—"

"I saw you yesterday, yes, but I am a detective," he offered as he showed her his badge. "I would like a few moments of your time."

She looked at him for several seconds before stepping aside and inviting him in with a sweep of her hand. As she closed the door Sutton had to admit that his first inside view of the house impressed him. The foyer was a cavern of high ceiling and soft lighting featuring what he considered an expensive area rug over cherry wood flooring. A deeply carpeted staircase on the right curved as it rose to the second floor

"Let's go into my office," Brenda invited, and Josh followed her to a door on the left. Her presence was elegance, something he had missed the previous day, but then again the circumstances were quite different today. Here she was in charge of the house and managing middle age well. She was no longer a tormented griever but rather a poised woman who had made peace, at least temporarily, with her new reality.

The detective did not see the children as he followed. Once inside the office he was somewhat surprised that the room was less than tidy. The work desk was covered with several files, an open book, a laptop and a plate containing the remnants of a meal. There was a wall totally covered with shelved books.

She removed a large shopping bag from one of the chairs facing the desk and invited him to sit. "Sorry about the mess. The last couple of days have not been ... usual. So, detective, what's this about?" she asked as she went to sit behind the desk.

"Dr. Castle, I am very sorry for your loss."

"Thank you."

"Your husband's body was released a few hours ago."

"I know. I just came from arranging the funeral."

"I am here to inform you of the results of the autopsy."

Her dark eyes looked straight into his. "He had a heart attack. That's what his doctor said."

"That's correct, but it was one brought on by something he had ingested."

"What? Are you saying he was poisoned?"

As she spoke he saw a quick flash cross her eyes. He took out his black notebook, opened it and flipped a page while analyzing her response. "It would appear so, ma'am. He was given aconite. Do you know it?"

"Why would I? I don't deal in poison!" she exclaimed.

"It's a type of neurotoxin he consumed in his coffee or in food."

"Where would one get ..."

"Aconite. It's derived from a plant called monkshood. It's very toxic."

She looked out the window briefly. "Could Murray have taken it by mistake?"

"Doubtful. It's not something readily available so it's very unlikely it could have been an accident."

"What about suicide?"

"Any specific reason why you ask that question? I mean, had his mood changed lately? Was he despondent, depressed?"

"He was less communicative. I thought he might have been having an affair."

"Did he exhibit signs that he could kill himself?"

"No, but I know that some people who take their own lives do not exhibit any sign of depression."

"I see," the detective commented briefly. After a moment of total silence hanging heavily in the room, Sutton continued. "Dr. Castle, as a result of the autopsy, your husband's death has now become a homicide investigation. So I need to ask you a few questions."

"Oh, I see. When there's a murder family members are always the first suspects, isn't that the case, detective?"

"It's a possibility we always have to investigate." He continued. "How long had you and your husband been married?"

"We would have been together twenty-eight years in June. We were planning to celebrate sometime this summer."

"You were aware that he was being sued—"

"Of course, like everyone else in Toronto. A lawyer getting into trouble is always good fodder for gossip."

"How did you feel about it?"

"What do you think? I felt embarrassed that my husband proved himself to be less than honest although he denied doing anything wrong."

"That legal action must have affected your marriage?"

"Well, I loved Murray and I stood by him."

"I take it you were nevertheless displeased, shall we say."

"Of course, but that's marriage. I loved him and supported him."

"You are a psychologist," Sutton said matter-of-factly.

"I have a PhD in psychology, yes. I am in private practice but I also see patients in a hospital setting from time to time for evaluation purposes."

The detective who had been jotting notes in his notebook lifted his head. "In the course of obtaining your degree, were poisons part of your studies?"

Her dark eyes darted at him. "You think I killed Murray?"

"Ma'am, I'm investigating and that includes taking a close look at family members. Did you?"

"Did I what? Study poisons? No sir. I did not. It's not a subject that interests me. Are we done here?"

Sutton said yes.

"Next, you'll want to talk to my children about that, no doubt."

"Yes. I'd like to see them one at a time."

Brenda stood up and told Sutton she would send them in.

A few moments later, Sally appeared. She had her mother's reddish hair and her eyes showed that she had been crying. "What do you want to know, detective? My dad had a heart attack. Why are you bothering us?"

"I'm sure your mother will elaborate on the real cause of death. How did you get along with your dad?"

"He was my hero," she said firmly, and Sutton felt somewhat silly to be interviewing the daughter who was obviously in pain.

"A nice way to describe your love for your father," Sutton commented, adding: "That's all for now."

Sally left the room and Brenda came back in. "You'll find my son at his office. He left just after you arrived."

"Thank you for your time, Dr. Castle. I may have to talk to you again," he said as he stood to leave.

Driving out of the subdivision, the detective's instincts were on full alert. Despite her denials, he had detected something in the woman's responses about the health of her marriage. Perhaps she was the one having the affair.

He had a lot more avenues to investigate.

The sky was cloudy and rain was promised for later in the day. Perfect weather for a funeral, Sutton thought. He was sitting in his unmarked sedan, at the outer end of the funeral home parking lot, his colleague Ross Walters at his side.

"Why are we here?" Ross asked. "We know from the obit online that the family wanted it to be a simple ceremony for family members only. Who do you expect to crash it? We've already seen two older couples, his parents and her parents no doubt. We've seen an assortment of middle-agers, surely aunts and uncles—"

"Where are Murray's partners and colleagues? We haven't talked to them yet, but I would recognize them from the photos I saw online."

"The guy was being sued by a client. Not positive PR. His colleagues must have been pissed. Why would they show up at his funeral?"

"Hello!" Sutton suddenly exclaimed as a tall man with a mess of dark hair splashed with white at the temples stepped out of the back of a large chauffeur-driven black SUV. "I know that fellow," he said.

"So do I. It's Joey Lacrosse. What's he doing here?"

"The plot thickens, That's the client suing Murray because he supposedly cost him money."

Ross could not help but whistle lightly.

The man, mid-fifties Sutton judged, walked up to the door of the funeral home with a determined walk then stopped. He was having second thoughts about meeting the family at this particular time, Sutton assumed. A hand went up to the door pull, but nothing happened. A moment later the man let go of the door pull, turned, walked back to his ride and got in.

"Cold feet or a sense of respect?" Walters asked.

"Your guess is as good as mine," Josh Sutton replied. "What do you say that after we check in with the captain you and I grab some lunch then go visit a law office?"

"Sounds good!'"

The two detectives were now approaching Marshall Road in their cruiser, a large bag resting on detective Walters lap. Sutton turned into the dead end road and parked a short distance in.

"When you talked about lunch, I had no idea we would be eating in such a wonderful atmosphere," Walters said. "You can't get enough of this area, can you?"

"It's quiet. Nothing on either side of the road but the land belonging to the Marshalls. A good place to think."

"Josh, perhaps you do too much of that," Ross said as he began distributing the food and drinks from the bag. "But then again ...."

"Maybe you're right, but how can I not think about Bryan and Anna? They're always with me."

"I know, buddy," Ross said as he attacked a large salad.

They ate in silence for a long while.

"Some days I wonder if I'll ever have a normal life again," Josh offered. "I've lost my family and I've yet to find directions to guide me to peace."

As he always did when Josh questioned the harsh blow life had thrown at him, Ross saw the wisdom of remaining quiet to let his colleague get the pain and fear off his chest. Wasn't that the way toward peace for his friend?

"Of course, I realize full well that I'm not the only one the virus saw fit to attack. Many families have lost loved ones. I know that, and I'm sure they're dealing with a lot of emotions, just like me. How are they coping? Are we all going to be able to resume our lives and cherish our memories? To see a rainbow of peace?" Josh Sutton said. Then after taking a sip of his drink, added: "Sorry, Ross. I didn't mean to throw it all your way."

"Nothing to be sorry about. You have to talk about your pain if you're to get past it. You can let it out my way any time."

Suddenly, a small black SUV with tinted windows sped past the cruiser on its way up the road. In a moment it was slowing down as it continued on. The two detectives waited with interest as the vehicle soon managed to turn around, come back down and drive out in the direction from which it had come.

"Congratulations, my friend. Another nefarious transaction averted. You are doing a lot to clean up crime," Ross said.

"Well, I might be simply sweeping it to another location. The parties in the SUV are surely on their phone arranging another location for a meet."

"Or maybe they're simply cancelling the whole thing," Ross said hopefully.

"And you dream in colour, no doubt," Josh stated.

CHAPTER FIVE

The receptionist smiled her bright smile when the two detectives entered the offices of Mercer Davis Carroll and Castle. "How may I help you today?"

"I assume Mr. Mercer is back from his trip," Josh commented.

"Got back a short time ago. Let me tell him you're here."

"I would prefer you didn't," Sutton offered. "Which way?"

As they followed the instructions from the receptionist the two detectives did not see the lawyer's assistant at her desk but the door to Gabriel Mercer's office was open. Josh knocked softly on the door frame. "Mr. Mercer?"

A nearly bald man in his sixties sitting behind a large ornate desk lifted his head. "That's right. How can I help you?"

The two detectives walked in, showed their badges and asked for a few minutes of his time.

"What is this about? One of our cases?"

"Afraid not. We're here with regard to the death of Murray Castle," Josh said.

"I don't understand. Murray had a heart attack."

"That's correct, but it was brought on by a poison. The killer no doubt expecting that the doctor who pronounced him dead would miss it."

"What? I can't believe that! Murray was a nice guy. Who would want to kill him?"

"The people he defrauded, perhaps," Walters stated.

"Detectives, the facts are not exactly as reported in the media. Murray was being sued but he would have won." The lawyer then seemed to remember his manners. "Why don't you gentlemen sit."

After the two detectives had comfortably settled in the two chairs facing the desk, Sutton spoke. "Perhaps someone here who felt Castle had betrayed the firm."

"You're not accusing me or other lawyers in this firm of killing Murray, are you?"

"We're simply investigating. Where were you when Mr. Castle died?"

"I was in Montreal on an important case. I came back this morning. I was hoping to attend Murray's funeral but got into Toronto too late. I wanted to fly back last evening, but air travel is no longer what it used to be, is it? Before the pandemic scared all of us there were flights at least every hour between Montreal and Toronto. No longer the case."

"None of the other lawyers in your firm attended the funeral?"

"No. Brenda, Mrs. Castle, wanted the funeral to be private."

Ross Walters spoke. "Mr. Mercer, we would like to take a look at Mr. Castle's files."

"Detective, our files are confidential .... of course, if you only want to know things like the names of any clients who were critical of Murray or clashed with him, you could talk to his paralegal and his assistant. I'm certain they would be able to answer your questions. Let me get them for you," Mercer said as he picked up the black office phone on his desk.

Arrangements were quickly made, and Walters stood up. "What about the Joey Lacrosse file?"

"I've got that. I can tell you anything you want to know."

A woman in her thirties of obvious Indian descent whose curls framed a lovely face appeared at the door. Mercer spoke. "Cecilia, this is the detective. You and Conrad should answer his questions. Ensure confidentiality."

"Of course, sir."

Ross Walters followed the woman out into the corridor.

"Anything else, detective?" Mercer asked Josh.

"Yes. I do have a few questions. You and Mr. Castle were partners?"

"That's right. After Murray passed the bar, he approached our small firm for a job. We took him on. We being myself and my wife who is also a lawyer. Murray was intelligent and a quick learner. We were both pleased with his work.

"About five years or so later, my wife decided to join a group of female lawyers representing exclusively female clients. I supported her because I thought it would benefit both of us."

"Did you get into a partnership with Murray Castle at that point?"

"No. There were other partners then and other lawyers in the firm with more experience than Murray. But over the years there were many changes. Some lawyers left to start their own firm, a partner died of cancer, and so on. In any event Murray was invited into a partnership about fifteen years or so ago now. Murray is ... was a very likeable fellow and attracted a lot of clients. It has worked very well for the firm that has been growing ever since and continues to attract a lot of lawyers as associates."

"Tell me about Joey Lacrosse," Josh Sutton asked simply.

Mercer closed his eyes for a moment as if he wished he didn't have to discuss that client. "Would you like some coffee, detective? I certainly could use some."

"Not for me, thank you, but you go ahead."

Mercer picked up the phone for his order, and soon a young man came into the office to put a ceramic mug in front of the lawyer.

"Mac, please close the door on your way out," Mercer asked, and the young man nodded and did as he was told.

Mercer took a couple of sips from the mug before speaking. "I think most people in Toronto have heard the name Joey Lacrosse. As you know he's a very wealthy developer and builder. He became a client of the firm soon after Murray made partner. Murray handled the man's legal affairs, his contracts, and so on. It was a lucrative file for us as you can imagine because Joey has a hand in a whole bunch of properties around town. Confidentially, the man does not always pay his bills on time preferring to invest that money into his business for as long as possible, something that irritated Murray.

"Two years ago or so, I guess, one of Joey's exes decided she needed more money than the settlement the pair had reached at the time of the divorce. She wanted to sue him. His wealth had grown substantially since their divorce and she felt entitled to a piece of the pie. It was clear, as far as Murray was concerned, that the woman expected Joey to settle with, shall we say, a sizeable donation to avoid legal complications."

Josh had been listening with interest and waited while Mercer got to his coffee one more time before continuing. "Joey then talked to Murray about putting a sizeable portion of his capital into an asset protection trust so it would be out of reach from the 'greedy bitch' as Joey qualified his former wife. So, a trust was created and the funds entrusted to our firm. Joey was billed accordingly, but ignored paying the invoice despite numerous requests from Murray.

"Months and months later, as a last resort, Murray approached Lacrosse about dipping into the trust fund so our firm could be paid. That riled Lacrosse who let the world know that Murray couldn't be trusted. He, Lacrosse, was in charge of the trust. Period. But, reluctantly, Lacrosse finally paid his bill in full, and somehow he and Murray turned over a new leaf because Lacrosse liked Murray's work on his behalf."

"You mean that Murray Castle continued to handle Mr. Lacrosse's legal affairs?"

"Correct. Not that unusual."

"But I understand Lacrosse is suing your firm, Murray Castle in particular, for millions."

"True, but it's just to flex his muscles, to prove himself. He won't get a penny."

"What was the reason for the legal action?"

Mercer explained that one day Lacrosse asked Castle to prepare a bid for a piece of land in the north end of the city that had come on the market and that Lacrosse wanted in order to build another exclusive condo building. Murray had heard a rumour about the land and tried to convince his client not to bid. They went back and forth about it for days until another developer acquired the piece of land. Lacrosse was livid and blamed Murray. He contacted another lawyer to sue him for the money he lost.

"But Murray was not worried," Mercer continued, "because he had done the right thing and saved Lacrosse tons of money and aggravation because by then he had had concrete confirmation that the land in question was contaminated. He tried to explain it all to Lacrosse but the man was not convinced. Then the pandemic hit and along with countless other legal actions the case has been in limbo ever since."

"You agreed that Castle did the right thing even if you are facing legal action?"

"Of course. Murray was an honest man."

"Is there any way Lacrosse can benefit from Castle's passing?"

"Not that I can see. On the contrary, he has to start all over with someone else. Bound to cause headaches all around."

"Tell me, did Mr. Castle have life insurance?" Sutton asked.

"Of course. He had a one million partner policy, as I and all the other partners do. The firm will benefit. It's standard practice."

"Do you know if he had other life insurance?"

"Well, he had a personal policy which Brenda will get. I believe it's also one million, but I'd have to check."

Josh Sutton stood up. "I appreciate your time, Mr. Mercer."

"Call me any time if you need more information."

"I want to talk to your partners. Where is Mr. Davis' office?"

"Arthur has the office at the end of the hall on the right."

CHAPTER SIX

Sutton thanked the lawyer and, closing the office door behind him, made his way down the hall. He saw Cecilia, Castle's assistant, at her desk a little ways down the hall, busy on the phone. He waited until she was finished. "I'm detective Sutton. You met with detective Walters?"

"I answered all the questions as best as I could."

"I'm sure you did, but I have one myself. The day he died, where and with whom did Murray Castle have lunch?"

"Just a second," she said as her fingers danced on the keyboard. "He did not have a lunch appointment. I was out for a couple of hours that day because of a dental appointment, so I'm afraid I don't know where he ate. Sorry."

"That's okay. When he did not have an appointment, where did he normally eat?"

"He often ordered a salad from the deli on the ground floor and ate at his desk while he checked the news. But I can't say for sure that's what he did the day he had the heart attack."

"Did your boss drink the coffee made here in the office, or did he or you get it outside?"

"Mr. Castle drank the coffee here. He didn't like outside specialty coffees because he thought they had too much sugar in them."

Josh thanked Cecilia and saw Ross Walters thanking a young man then walking towards him. The two detectives made their way down the hall to the office of Arthur Davis. His assistant was engrossed in reading a document and didn't look up until Sutton spoke. After introducing themselves and showing their badges, the detectives were ushered into the lawyer's office.

The room was large with lots of windows that looked onto a wide view of downtown Toronto in the distance. The man himself was about the same age as Gabriel Mercer, in his sixties. He had thinning grey hair which contrasted with his ruddy complexion.

The assistant introduced the two detectives before leaving.

"What is this about?"

"We're investigating the death of Murray Castle."

"Murray had a heart attack. What's there to investigate?" Davis wanted to know.

"He did have a heart attack however it was caused by a poison he ingested."

"What? You mean he was murdered?"

"Correct. Tell us about your relationship with Mr. Castle," Sutton asked.

"You think I could have killed him? I'm a barrister, for heaven's sake, I stand for justice in the courts. I am not a murderer. Besides I liked Murray, He was a great guy and an asset to the firm. Everyone felt the same about him."

"Obvious someone did not," Walters offered.

Sutton asked: "Did you and Castle socialize outside the office?"

"My wife and I had dinner at Murray and Brenda's house on occasion. All the partners did. And vice versa. We all got along well." He took a breath then asked: "You mean someone here in this office could be a murderer?"

"Most probably."

On hearing the reply, Davis closed his eyes. When he opened them again, Sutton had the impression that the lawyer was expecting he'd be waking up from a dream. But the detective considered that murderers were devious and that it could be an act.

"Our investigation will continue and we will get back to you if we have more questions," Sutton said.

Davis seemed relieved to see that they were leaving. The surviving partners would no doubt engage in conjectures of all sorts until the culprit was identified, Sutton thought.

Walters asked Davis' assistant the way to the office of Constance Carroll.

"Ms. Carroll is away for a while. She underwent surgery," the woman answered.

"What type of surgery?"

"We were told that she didn't want to talk about her operation expect for the fact that it was not especially serious."

"When did she have the surgery?"

"The day after poor Mr. Castle died."

"You liked Mr. Castle?" Sutton asked.

"Very much. He was nice. Always had a good word to say to us the assistants. Not like... Never mind. I didn't say anything."

"Of course not," Sutton encouraged. "Do you know when Ms. Carroll will be back in the office."

"No, I don't. The receptionist would."

On their way out, the detectives learned that Ms. Carroll would be away for another week.

The two detectives made their way back to their car in silence. Once they were on the road, Detective Walters reported his findings to his partner.

The younger detective reported that essentially all the associate lawyers liked the personable Castle. Many of them sought his expertise for some of their cases and had only praise for his generosity in sharing his time and experience.

As for Castle's clients, according to his paralegal and his assistant, none of them had ever criticized the lawyer. And that went for current as well as past clients. Castle's cases were mostly related to business, contracts, and the like. No criminal cases.

"It seems that none of the personnel in the office had any reason for harming Castle," Ross concluded.

"That we know of so far," Josh replied. "From my research last night I figure that the killer went to a lot of trouble to find the perfect poison, something that could kill Castle in a short period of time if he ingested enough. And a poison that could only be identified if there was an autopsy which the killer believed would not happen. He was certain everyone would think Castle died from a cardiac issue. Very clever but also very premeditated. An intelligent person with a definite motive. We find the motive, we find the killer."

"Nothing to it," Ross said.

CHAPTER SEVEN

The sun was almost totally disappearing by the time Josh drove west into a nearby suburb. He turned when he saw the white sign with just one name: Montrose. He made his way between two white pillars into the driveway of a baronial-esque three-story white structure that had once been the home of a wealthy Ontario family. It now had two extensions at the back and served as a private mental hospital. He parked in the area on the side of the house which had once been a lush lawn but was now paved and reserved for visitors.

The guard on duty nodded as Sutton entered through the elegant front door and was greeted by the warm smile of the familiar young woman seated in front of a large screen at the semi circular counter. "Good evening, detective. How are you?"

"Not bad, considering," he replied as he made his way up a large staircase.

As he began walking down the hall of the second floor, he saw the imposing Greta coming toward him, as she always did when he came. He knew, of course, that the receptionist never failed to notify the fifty-something heavyset Greta of his arrival. Despite her somewhat stern appearance it was clear to him that the head nurse at the private facility had a soft spot for him and his wife. Pity, no doubt, but clearly she wanted to do as much as possible to ease their burden. She was an angel who had taken Anna Sutton under her wing something for which Josh would always be grateful.

"Nice to see you, detective. We're very pleased that your wife is improving every day," the nurse stated. "I believe Dr. Maxwell expect a full recovery very soon."

"Great news, but I don't want to get my hopes up. Not yet, at least."

"Understandable."

"Greta, may I ask you something? Do you know a Dr. Brenda Castle?"

"Yes. Dr. Castle sees patients here from time to time." She lowered her voice: "At the moment she tends to a rich kid who's here incognito. She is a psychologist, not a psychiatrist like Dr. Maxwell."

"When is she here?"

"Not sure off hand, but I could find out."

He put his hand in his inside jacket pocket of his suit jacket and pulled out his information card. "I'd really appreciate it. My numbers. Just leave a message. And, please, this is just between us!"

"Detective, I am always on your side," she said sincerely as she took the card.

Josh thanked the nurse and made his way to a door at the end of the hall. He knocked very softly before pulling the handle down, pushing the door, stepping inside the large room and closing the door behind him.

His heart leapt to his throat as it always did when he saw her, partly due to joy and partly due to pain. She was seated in her maroon armchair by the window, reading a book. She was wearing the satiny pink robe he had gotten her as a birthday gift in March, and he saw that her dark blond hair had been styled away from her face, the way he liked it. And to make it a good day all around he saw that her hands were not gloved.

Still a beautiful creature!

She looked up and her face immediately exploded with joy. "Josh! You've finished work!"

"For today." He bent down and kissed her cheek. "How are you, honey?"

"I'm just fine. I can't wait to go home."

He pulled one of the chairs reserved for visitors to her side, and sat down. He took her hand into his, grateful for the softness.

"I can go home, Josh. I don't wash my hands much now. I wash them after going to the bathroom, of course."

"I know. You told me and that's why your hands are very soft."

"It's the nice lotion you got me," she said, smiling. "Oh, Josh, I want to go home. I don't cry anymore … not all the time."

"I am aware of that, but do you know why you cry so often?"

"Because I'm sad."

"Why are you sad?"

She pulled her hand away from his. "Don't talk to me like I'm a child, Josh. You know I cry because I miss Bryan and no one tells me when he'll be back. That's why I cry."

He wanted to tell her that their child would never be back, that he had been one of the very few young children the pandemic had seen fit to attack and destroy, but he still did not have the courage. Anna was still too fragile.

"Did you talk to Jenny today?"

"Yes. I do every day. I miss not being with her at the studio. I miss our clients."

"Well, you'll be able to get back to them soon."

There was a knock on the door to which Anna said it was open. A middle-age man with salt and pepper hair stepped into the room.

"Hello, Dr. Maxwell. Did I miss an appointment?" Anna asked.

"No. Not at all. I just came to see if you needed anything."

"No, thank you. I'm fine. You know my husband Josh."

Josh stood up and the two men shook hands.

"Of course. Nice to see you again, detective," the doctor offered. "I saw Anna teaching yoga to two patients today. I was very impressed."

"When can I go back to my studio and take care of my regular clients?"

"Very, very soon, I promise," Dr. Maxwell said to Anna. Turning to Josh, he added: "I have paperwork to get through this evening. After your visit with Anna perhaps you could drop by my office. I've moved to number 10, still on the first floor."

"Happy to."

"Dr. Maxwell, I want to go home," Anna stated firmly.

"I don't blame you. Married to a detective must be very interesting."

"It is, and Josh is the best husband in the world."

Dr. Maxwell approached Anna and put a hand on her shoulder.

"As we discussed, you can't go home just yet, not until we can find out what happened to Bryan. Otherwise it could be dangerous."

Reluctantly, she said: "I understand. It won't take long to find out, will it?"

"No. We're almost there," the therapist said with a smile. "Have a good visit with Josh and we'll talk tomorrow. Sleep well."

Detective Josh Sutton was pleased with Dr. Maxwell's assessment of Anna's progress. The two men were seated in comfortable armchairs in the psychiatrist's office.

"I think your wife is on the threshold of seeing the grim reality for herself. I believe she understands that a very important element of her life is about to be revealed. Of course, it'll be very traumatic, but the healing will only be able to begin once she faces the trauma. We will all be there for her." A moment later, Dr. Maxwell continued. "What about you? How are you doing?"

"Every day's a bit easier, I suppose. I've got to blame someone, something, so I blame the virus all the time. It seems to help."

"Good for you for finding an outlet. So many souls were devastated by the pandemic. You lost a child to it. There is no greater loss in this life. And you had to deal with your wife's innovative way of shielding herself from a pain she was unable to face."

"Why did she react that way?"

"We are far from knowing all there is to know about the mind, just like we don't know everything about the body. Why do some people get cancer and others don't even when they have the same lifestyle? Simply put, we can never be totally sure."

"How long do you think before I can take Anna home?"

"A timeframe in these situations is always a bit tricky. She has now accepted that the virus is no longer a threat and that washing her hands a hundred times a day is a not normal. That's a great step forward. But it'll be baby steps to full acceptance of her loss."

"This is not her studio, but teaching yoga here must be good for her," Josh stated.

"I believe it's a great help, both physically and emotionally, on her way toward healing."

"I'm very grateful for all you do for Anna"

"Your wife is a very easy to care for."

"Doctor, can I ask you something on a totally different subject?"
"Of course."
"Why do regular people, not psychopaths, murder other people?"
"How much time have you got?"
Josh Sutton smiled slightly.

CHAPTER EIGHT

Everything and everyone around him in the division was quiet early the next morning as detective Josh Sutton was at his desk in his office with a cup of coffee in front of him. He was in full analyzing mode as he reviewed the progress of the case. So far, despite his efforts and those of detective Walters, it had only been information gathering with little headway in identifying possible Murray Castle murderers.

The case certainly needed an approach that differed from other murder cases he had investigated. There was no physical evidence of any kind. No murder weapon, no gun to identify, no bullets to dust for prints, no knife to examine, no blunt object to ascertain, no fingerprints to spot, no fibres to unearth, no footprints to examine, no tire marks to discover, no DNA under fingernails to catch, and no blood splatters to study. It had been a quiet murder. And the murderer need not have been close to Castle not even in the same office or even the same city.

Exactly how it was delivered was the question. It could have been in coffee since that was found in his stomach by the coroner along with food. That meant that since the death occurred in the afternoon he had probably ingested the derivative from monkshood at lunch. Although that was simply a deduction which could very well have no merit.

Sutton's instincts told him that Gabriel Mercer would have supported Castle all the way to the supreme court if need be because he judged his partner as having done the right, honest thing. Appearances were not always was they seemed, Sutton considered. Could there have been a more personal reason for Mercer to want Castle out of the way?

What about the other lawyers in the firm? Each of them needed closer examination than the brief one Walters had conducted.

The detective wondered why Brenda Castle seemed so affected by her late husband's actions while his partner saw it as something that needed to be lauded.

Two viewpoints, a tale of two cities!

His thoughts were suddenly interrupted by his captain. "Good morning, Josh. Got a minute?"

"Sure," Josh replied and followed Captain Corbett into his office.

"How are you doing, Josh? I mean really."

"I'm okay. *Petit train va loin.*"

"I'm not as bilingual as you. What does it mean?"

"Basically, slowly but surely. You know, captain, there's no need for you to worry that I can't do my job properly."

"I know you do excellent work. I just want to make sure you take care of yourself."

"I do. I run most mornings and I see my therapist every second week now."

"Glad to hear it. Keep it up. How's Anna doing?" Corbett asked as he settled at his desk.

"A little better, but she still asks why our little Bryan's not back."

"It's amazing how people are still suffering the effects of the pandemic. You like the facility where she is?"

"It's great! The staff's devoted to her and the psychiatrist keeps me informed of her progress. Captain, again I am so very grateful that you saw to it that she could get in there."

"You know, our government was very committed to helping Canadians financially during the crisis. I just made sure that our law enforcement personnel and their spouses could access some of that generosity. The special benefit took a while to materialize, but your wife's now getting appropriate care in a controlled environment and liberating you from worry. I'm glad it's all working out."

"Again, I'm very grateful."

" Anything to report on the Castle murder?"

"Not yet, unfortunately. We have only been gathering information at this point."

"Keep me informed," the captain said.

"Of course," Josh replied as he left.

Captain Corbett felt for his detective. The poor man's grieving was still ongoing. As he often did, Corbett wished he had a magic wand so things could go back to the way they were prior to the pandemic. He sighed knowing full well that the world had changed and would never fully recover for everyone. A new reality had settled in. He himself had lost his mother who had been in a senior care home, and because he could not be with her she had died alone. His thoughts of her were still painfully mixed with guilt, although he could not be faulted for obeying the rules.

But the home where she resided would be faulted. He had joined with others who had lost a parent in a class action suit against the private residence where deeply disturbing care issues had been detected. It seemed to him that the more senior care cost, the greater the number of patients who had succumbed during the pandemic. The provincial government had already elaborated new rules for all care facilities, including the private ones. He had heard that these new rules were already implemented in the residence where his mother had been a patient, however that did not give them a free pass.

The owners still had to be held accountable for all the worry and pain relatives of the deceased had had to endure.

Like him, people had been shaken to the core and the scars ran deep. The future was now one of hidden angst and careful planning as adjustments were still being assessed. Corbett knew the trepidation could very well be permanent for his generation.

Detective Sutton arrived early at the University of Toronto for his appointment with the expert on toxins recommended by Castle's physician. He made his way to the room number where they were to meet, and Sutton saw that a handwritten name which read 'Professor Blanchard' had been taped to the door.

A short while later, a very tall man in his late forties wearing jeans with a leather jacket that had seen better days approached, briefcase in hand. He wore a Blue Jays baseball cap on his head. "Detective Sutton?"

"That's right."

"Joe Blanchard. Hope you didn't have to wait too long."

"Not at all."

The man unlocked his door and invited the detective to follow him inside the somewhat small space. "Sit, sit," he told Josh. "How may I help you?"

Both men sat, and Sutton spoke. "As I told you on the phone, Dr. Hewell recommended you. I'm investigating a homicide involving poison and would like your input. May I ask about your background?"

"Of course. I am a medical doctor. I always had a desire to pursue research, so after my internship I did turn to research. I work for a large lab on a variety of projects for the government. Toxicology is only one of those."

"You do teach here at the university?"

"Yes. I teach research protocols. It's a part-time gig. I like it because researchers like myself need to interact with people so we don't go bonkers!" the doctor said with a mischievous grin.

"But you do know a lot about poisons?"

"I do. I've studied poisons and have analyzed them. What exactly do you want to know?"

"Anything you can tell me about a specific poison: aconite."

"Ha! Aconitum. It's an extract from a wild flower that grows here as well as in other countries."

"How would a person know it?"

"It's recognized by its blue or purple flowers that are somewhat shaped like helmets."

"But it is poisonous?"

"It's a cardio toxin which means that it can paralyze the heart muscle and cause death."

"You would have to know how to prepare the poison from the flower, right?"

"Certainly. However, herbalists work with both the flowers and the roots. In Asian culture aconite has some medicinal uses, one of them being to combat pain, but herbalists make sure it is safe to ingest."

"Could someone simply pick the flower, dry it and use it as a poison?"

"It's not that simple. Monkshood, the flower, is very nasty. Just brushing against the petals can cause serious problems. A person would have to have some training to prepare it properly, otherwise it'd be dangerous."

"Would someone taking aconite in food taste it?"

"Very much so. It has a rather sharp bitter taste that provokes a burning sensation."

"I take it a person would need to ingest a lot of it to be poisoned."

"Not really. It is quite toxic. Ingesting even a small amount that has not been properly prepared could cause problems. I take it you have a case involving aconite?"

"Correct. I'm trying to find out how the man could ingest enough of a dose to die from it. I mean, he died in his office in the afternoon so the poison had to have been introduced in his system a few hours earlier, at lunch perhaps, without him tasting it."

"I'm afraid that couldn't have been possible. A fatal dose would have had almost immediate results," Blanchard concluded.

Sutton realized that his deduction that Murray Castle ingested aconite at lunch was wrong. What other explanation was there? Someone at the law office had to have given Castle a dose shortly before he collapsed. But how?

The detective thanked Blanchard and left. He had a great deal of work ahead of him.

Back in his car, Sutton called the office of the main pathologist. He spoke briefly with the doctor who had done the post-mortem on Murray Castle and got the answer he expected. He then spoke with his colleague Ross Walters. The two men agreed on what needed to be done. Now there was a plan. A definite plan. Both men wondered why they had not made the connection before.

A bit later, Sutton was again at the Castle home. He could not ring the doorbell before Walters arrived with the warrant. There was only one car parked near the house: the classic VW which, according to his research, belonged to the daughter, Sally. That meant that Brenda Castle was not home. Perhaps that was a good omen.

He got out of the vehicle and stretched. With the nice house in the background and the sun shining in the quiet warming air, it was the perfect setting for meditation. His efforts at concentrating on only one aspect of his life at a time so that his harsh reality did not overwhelm him were paying dividends. He could now easily guide his mind to complete relaxation where he always saw his son Bryan's happy and beautiful face. There was no pain, only the joy and gratitude of having been his father for six years. That realization would never fade. It would be with him the rest of his life.

He was enjoying the memory of Bryan's curiosity on his first day of school when Walters' arrival brought him out of his *rêverie.*

The two men walked up to the door and rang the bell. Sally answered.

"Hello. We would like to come inside."

"My mother's not here right now, detective. She's working. What exactly do you want?"

"We need to examine the clothes your dad was wearing when he died. The coroner's office sent them here."

"I don't know anything about that. Come in," she finally invited.

The detectives stepped inside as Sally closed the door. Sutton spoke: "A package was delivered here perhaps just before the funeral."

"I have no idea. I'll ask Con," she said and disappeared through a door.

A moment later she returned with a woman who was clearly of Mexican descent. "This is Consuela. She says that a package arrived a couple days ago."

"Did you open it?" Josh asked the woman.

"No. It's for Mrs. Castle. I give it to her when she is better."

"I would like to see it," Josh stated.

Now Sally objected. "No can do, detective. Not without a warrant," the lawyer's dutiful daughter emphasized.

Walters put a hand in the inside pocket of his jacket and retrieved a warrant he presented to Sally. She looked at it briefly and sighed. "Show them," she said to Consuela.

In the well-appointed kitchen, the Mexican woman opened a large cupboard door and pointed to a package wrapped in brown paper and tied with cord. Sutton picked it up and put it on a small table near a window. He put on gloves, and with Walters and the two women watching, he opened it.

Slowly he pulled out a small bag containing Murray Castle's wallet, a set of keys, and a few dollars in loose change. That was followed by another bag in which there was a pair of fine Italian black loafers. Next came an expensive dark blue silk suit. Sutton pulled out the jacket and checked all the pockets. In the inside one there was a small plastic pillbox containing a capsule of white powder and two other round lilac-coloured tablets that reminded him of the vitamin C pills he took regularly. Sutton carefully put the pillbox inside an evidence bag he pulled from one of his pockets.

The search had been worthwhile!

"Did your dad take medication?" Sutton asked Sally.

She was adamant that her dad did not take any meds.

"So, what's this then?" Sutton continued.

"Vitamins," Consuela said. "Mr. Castle put it in that box in the morning before going to the office."

"What kind of vitamin?"

Consuela opened one of the cupboard doors where several bottles of various vitamins were neatly aligned.

"We'll have to take all these," Sutton said.

Consuela objected. "No. Mrs. Castle take some every morning."

"Well, she'll have to do without for a few days."

On their way to Murray Castle's law office, the two detectives stopped at the division. They dropped off the small plastic pillbox found inside the pocket of Murray Castle's suit jacket. They asked for forensics to examine it for fingerprints as well as thoroughly examine the contents with regard to aconite.

They were told the results would be forthcoming.

CHAPTER NINE

Malcolm Castle was busy taking down mementos and frames from the walls of his father's office when detective Sutton knocked lightly on the door frame, Walters close behind. The young man looked up. "Yes?"

"Malcolm Castle?"

"That's right. Who are you? How did you get pass reception?"

The two detectives showed their badges. Sutton spoke. "We're the detectives assigned to your father's case. Mr. Mercer is aware that we are here and that we have a warrant to search this office."

Malcolm, who was certain his father had not been murdered, was shocked. He sat down behind the desk. "It's outrageous. You can't be serious! You actually think that my dad was murdered like some ... hood. He was a good man who helped a lot of people ..."

"We're sorry for your loss, Mr. Castle, but autopsies don't lie. He was poisoned. We understand that it's difficult for you to accept our findings, but I repeat that autopsies don't lie. We came to search your father's office for any possible clues, so please stop what you're doing so we can look around."

"I don't believe it. Whoever did the autopsy must have made a mistake. Dad had a heart attack. I know. I was with him when it happened."

Sutton said. "What exactly did happen?"

"I was here in his office. We were discussing a case I was handling when all of a sudden he didn't look well. He picked up his wastepaper basket and vomited into it. I thought it must have been something he ate at lunch. Then he put a hand to his chest and fell forward. I yelled for help, for someone to call Dr. Hewell here in the building. Then I tried mouth-to-mouth resuscitation for a while but it didn't do anything."

"Had you eaten lunch with your father?"

"No. I ordered something in and worked on my case. I don't know where dad ate.""Did your father eat or drink anything while you were with him?"

Malcolm's shoulders went up briefly. "No."

"Are you quite certain?"

"Yeah. Pretty much."

"Did your father smoke?"

"Never."

"Did anyone come into his office while you were with him prior to him collapsing?"

"You mean another lawyer?" Malcolm looked out the window momentarily. "I don't think so. No one, I'm sure."

"The shock of seeing your father in distress must have been quite upsetting." The detective paused for a moment before continuing. "You were aware that your father had some legal problems, were you not?"

"Of course, but he didn't do anything wrong. He only acted in the best interest of the client. He would have won the litigation."

Josh Sutton thought how great it was to be young and to believe that everything would work out as one wished. The young man would eventually learn, like the rest of the world, that life has a mind of its own, Josh mused.

"Right now I need to ask you to leave this room so we can do our job."

Reluctantly, Malcolm stood up and walked out.

Josh Sutton and Ross Walters went to work. Josh examined every drawer of Murray Castle's desk. His reasoning was that there could be some indication of the poison in the office since that's where Murray had ingested it. Sutton no longer doubted that was the case.

He waded through a variety of papers and files that seemed to be nearly organized but he didn't detect any vial or container of any sort. Murray's wife had hinted that he could have been having an affair, so Josh carefully examined under everything. In one of the drawers, under a pile of personal bills, he came upon an envelope with no indication as to its content. To the detective, through his gloves, it felt like a few sheets of paper. Sutton cautiously opened the unsealed envelope to reveal several hundred dollar bills. Almost a thousand dollars. "Why would Castle have that amount of cash in his desk?" Sutton asked Walters.

"Many people keep cash on hand for emergencies."

Sutton thought that might have been the case for Castle.

It took some time for the two detectives to examine the whole office. In the file cabinet, Walters did not detect any container of any sort. He had not really expected to find anything, but the investigation had to be thorough.

Finally, not finding anything, the two men removed their gloves and walked out of the office. Malcolm was looking especially sad as he sat near Cecilia's desk.

"We appreciate your time, Mr. Castle. You can go back inside."

Malcolm waved awkwardly as he stepped back into the space where his father had worked for so many years.

At that moment Sutton's phone buzzed. The caller was nurse Greta who said that Dr. Castle was at the hospital on an emergency. Friday was not her regular day. She usually came in on Monday mornings. Sutton thanked her.

Sutton then spoke to Cecilia. "Can you tell me if your boss kept any medication in his office."

"I know Mr. Castle did not take meds of any kind. He took vitamin C at this time of year because of seasonal allergies. When spring buds start to come out. He didn't want to take allergy medicine."

"Did he keep vitamins in the office?"

"He always had them in a small pillbox in the pocket of his jacket. Said it helped him."

"Do you know when he took vitamins?"

"I'm sorry, but I'm not sure."

"We didn't see any computer on Mr. Castle's desk. Did he not use one?"

"He used a laptop to keep up with the news and to do a bit of research, but he didn't enter any data. I did all the typing. He also had a phone, of course."

"Where is that phone? And that laptop?"

"Right here," Cecilia said as she opened a drawer in her desk.

"After they removed the body I thought it would be wise to take them for safe keeping."

"We'll take those if you don't mind," Sutton said.

She pulled out the two devices and gave them to the detective.

Sutton thanked her and the men made their way out.

As the detectives were in the elevator on their way to the garage, detective Sutton's phone buzzed. The call was from the police lab. "You have something for us?" he asked the chief.

"We tested all the bottles you left with us. Nothing but vitamins. Same for the two tablets in the plastic pillbox. As for the capsule in the pillbox, it's calcium which as you know people take for their bones. However, we found a microscopic amount of aconitum in there as well which means that the poison was present in the pillbox at some point. Can't say when though."

"Can aconite be made into a powder then put into a capsule shell that would look like the calcium one in the pillbox?"

"A capsule would have had a gelatine casing not likely to open. My money is on a compacted solid tablet. Either way you'd certainly have to know what you're doing. Not only is the substance dangerous, you'd have to know the exact proportions, etc. It would definitely take an expert."

"I was told aconite is very bitter which the victim would surely have tasted by putting the pill in his mouth."

"Any such tablet would have to have been coated with some sugary substance so it could be swallowed without tasting the poison."

"Then it could not be a regular MD?"

"Not unless he trained as an herbalist."

Exciting information, Sutton thought. He now knew how the poison was administered, but the main questions still had no answers: Who? Why?

The detectives went down to the basement garage of the building, with the keys Cecilia had given them, where they found Murray Castle's luxurious import. They carefully examined the interior as well as the trunk. The machine was obviously kept pristinely clean and the faint aroma of lavender was still clinging to the air.

"Must have been washed inside and out just before the guy left this world," Walters concluded.

"Certainly looks like it."

"He ingested poison in his office. I don't see the point of searching his car," Walters said.

"I know. But we do need to check everything. We do want to make sure no one questions this investigation. We're dealing with lawyers after all." Then Sutton pointed to a fellow working in a glass-enclosed office near the elevator.

Both men walked in that direction and the man stepped out. "Gentlemen, what can I do for you?"

Both detectives showed their badges, then Sutton asked: "Can those who use this parking get their cars washed?"

"Certainly," the man replied. "We have all the equipment out back. We wash both the outside and the inside, and vacuum the interior thoroughly. A guy who works maintenance in the building does it. "

"Do you remember when you last cleaned Murray Castle's BMW?"

"That's easy. The morning he died. Such a nice man. I still can't believe he's gone."

"Did he order the wash himself or did his assistant call you?"

"He asked me when he arrived in the morning. Said he was taking his wife out and wanted extra attention."

The detectives thanked the man and left.

Once they were back in their sedan, Sutton said: "Ross, since you're a technology expert, why don't you examine Castle's phone and laptop. See what turns up. Especially interested in any indication of an affair."

"You think he was cheating?"

"His wife seems to think so."

CHAPTER TEN

At home while eating pizza washed down with cold beer, Sutton was doing some research on his laptop at his dining room table. He needed more information. Who could prepare a capsule containing poison or make a poisoned pill that looked like a vitamin tablet? He didn't think anyone in Castle's entourage could.

Yet it had been done.

Sutton saw that naturopaths dealt in plants among other things. He examined the training required for a person to get a license and then read all about naturopaths. They essentially believed that nature provided the answers to the physical problems of mankind. They were convinced that plants could be used to replace traditionally produced pharmaceutical remedies, but surely that did not include aconite. For naturopaths it was a question of knowing how to use plants, but he saw no indication that they were herbalists as Doctor Blanchard at the university had qualified those who knew all about poisons.

As he read further, Sutton realized that people of all walks of life believed in the power of the body to heal itself through various treatments that alleviate physical problems. He saw that it included acupuncture, a treatment his own mother used every so often to manage her arthritic pain. Looking at the long list of practitioners Sutton saw that naturopathy was obviously big business in and around

Toronto. However he realized that the investigation had to follow another road leading to herbalists.

He knew he could find them in the Chinatown section of the city.

Could plants do anything to heal his dear Anna, he wondered for a second before dismissing the thought. He had never believed in miracles.

Murray Castle preferred vitamins over allergy medication so he could very well have consulted natural specialists to solve other problems. After all he was nearly fifty-five years old so he was bound to have required medical attention at one point or another. And he might not have consulted Dr. Hewell for everything. While at it, could Castle himself have ordered an aconite pill or capsule? Bold gesture if that were the case but it would mean the perfect suicide if he wanted to make certain his family did not know the real reason for his demise. His wife had hinted at that possibility. However there were lots of other ways for someone to take their life, so going the route that killed Murray Castle certainly seemed over-the-top complicated.

One way or another, a pill or capsule containing a fatal dose of aconite had been prepared to look like a simple vitamin. Someone with the right expertise had to have done it. Someone who could have been swayed to do it for a price. Josh Sutton had learned early in his career that when money was no object, anything and everything could be had.

Sutton spent the next morning contacting Asian herbalists by phone after checking their reviews online. He told them that he was looking into natural remedies for a chronically painful shoulder and wanted to have some indication of the help they could provide. The information that was discussed was basically the same from the three contacts, and most of the plant names that were discussed were totally unknown to Josh.

He asked them if they could prepare special mixtures from notes that his grandmother had written many years earlier. All of them seemed excited at the prospect of seeing such artisanal records, and said that there was no reason they couldn't prepare the described mixtures. Those answers didn't, however, indicate any proof that one of them had prepared or could prepare a poisonous pill or capsule.

But, Josh mused, some herbalists could be more receptive than others to preparing a poisonous pill. But how to go about finding such a culprit was the question. He needed to let this simmer in his mind for a while so he got busy with the laundry and other chores around the house that Anna had so lovingly decorated.

Stepping away from a problem for a bit often led to surprising answers.

At the end of the afternoon he was ready for a discussion with Ross Walters. The two met at Walters' house because the younger detective wanted to make sure Josh "ate a decent meal." Sutton very much appreciated the barbecued steak and veggies.

Ross Walters was busy digging into Murray Castle's phone history. He was looking into the lawyer's communications going backwards. The project was getting rather boring because the calls were basically all to his wife and two children. The texts were all dealing with mundane subjects from dinner reservations to invitation to a Maple Leafs hockey game.

He decided he had done enough for a Saturday, and put the phone aside.

CHAPTER ELEVEN

Josh woke up on Sunday morning to a glorious warming sunshine. He went for his usual run and could not help feeling that the day would be special. After a shower and a homemade smoothie, he felt good as he drove to his wife's hospital.

He had called her, and she was waiting in the foyer on the first floor. She wore a well-cut navy blazer over a new pair of soft jeans, the colour of her eyes, and a cream silk top. He smiled broadly as soon as he saw her and she responded with the joyful grin of a happy child.

He took her to brunch at her favourite spot: a restaurant on a small ship anchored in the harbour. She loved the array of choices at the elaborate buffet. That was happiness, he thought. Seeing his wife so very trouble free. For the time being, at least. The subject of their son did not come up in conversation as they enjoyed the delicious food offerings while taking in a magnificent view of Lake Ontario as well as of the skyline of downtown Toronto and the CN Tower, the tallest structure in Canada.

While they were sipping coffee, Anna surprised Josh with a question. How would he feel about having another child or two. "We're still young enough. Why not? What do you say?"

He looked into her eyes and there was a connection, the type of connection they used to share all the time. He knew then that she was well aware of their reality. She was simply not yet quite ready to express out loud that Bryan would not be back, Perhaps before she could accept and admit their reality she had to be able to let herself embrace life again. He considered that to her mind motherhood could probably be the ticket to life renewed.

By the time Josh drove Anna back in late afternoon, they had made the best of their time together while walking along the downtown streets and parks. Their conversation was about all the changes they would make to their suburban home. It was spring after all, a time of rebirth and new beginnings.

Josh was somewhat flabbergasted at the complete turn in Anna's view of life. Until then her remarks about the future had been simply bland. Resume life, continue crying. Now she had hope. Would it continue? Dr. Maxwell would no doubt have an answer.

On Monday morning, Josh Sutton drove out again to Montrose. After spending most of previous day with Anna, he needed answers to many questions. He had left a message for Dr. Maxwell about an urgent matter, and his phone buzzed as he was parking his car near the large house. The psychiatrist invited the detective to come right in.

Josh took his time to recount as accurately as possible his conversation with Anna while Dr. Maxwell listened without comment. "What do you think, doctor?"

The therapist was cautious. "This is obviously a big step forward. However she never discussed the idea of having children with me. Perhaps she needed to discuss it with you to see how you felt. I need time to assess this development. I am seeing her for a regular session this morning after her yoga class and should be able to give you my opinion soon. I will call you."

Josh offered his thanks then asked another question, totally unrelated. He had to advance the investigation into the Castle murder as quickly as possible and he still felt that there was something significant to unearth about the recent widow. "Doctor, do you know psychologist Brenda Castle?"

"I know who she is but I don't know her. I read that she lost her husband a few days ago. Do you want to see her as a patient?'

"No. I'm investigating her husband's murder."

"He was murdered? There was nothing about that in the media."

"We are keeping it quiet for the time being. Thank you for your time, doctor."

On leaving Maxwell's office, Josh went up to the second floor looking for nurse Greta but realized that she worked only later in the day. He went out to his car without looking in on Anna. It was the best course of action until he had more guidance from her therapist.

He sat in his car for a moment to organize his thoughts and his next move when, from the corner of his eyes, he saw Brenda Castle arrive in her white sedan. She parked several cars away from him and stayed put for a long moment as she talked on her phone.

Ever since he had seen her cry in her car he could not shake a feeling that something was not right. Had she really been crying for her husband that day? Or had she been crying for a completely different reason?

To be a good detective one had to be able to read people and Brenda certainly did not strike him as being the type to commit murder.

She ended her call and stepped out of the car. Looking at her make her way to the front door, he thought that she exhibited a definite slowness of movement compared to the sureness she had shown when he had seen her at home. Perhaps she was going back to work before having taken enough time to properly grieve.

In a moment she was disappearing inside the hospital.

As Sutton drove away, Brenda Castle got settled in the room she used to meet with patients at the private hospital. Soon, lanky denim-clad Garrett Perkins, nineteen years old, whose brown eyes matched his hair, came in and immediately slouched into an armchair. The mother in her wanted to scream that the young man should show more respect by sitting up properly, but that was not the reason for the session.

"How are you doing today, Garrett?"

"Fine."

"You know that you won't be able to leave here unless I give your parents assurances that you're willing to improve your behaviour and have already taken steps in that direction."

"I'm an adult. I don't have to listen to them."

"Well, lawyers of the man you attacked think so. You seriously injured your neighbour just for the fun of it."

"He was bugging me. He kept telling me to stop driving over his lawn, just like his lawn is special. It's just a fucking lawn!"

"Certainly, but it's his property. What prompted you to keep doing it despite his warnings?"

The teen didn't see the need to answer.

"You showed a lack of respect by continuing to drive over the lawn, but your tendency to violence came out when you stabbed the poor man. You could easily have killed him."

"He sounded like a broken record."

"Do you think that solving disputes by being physical is the answer to life's problems?"

Again, no comment.

"You're quite fortunate that your father was able to convince your neighbour not to press charges and that a stint of self improvement would make you a better person."

"Cut the crap, doctor. My father paid the idiot neighbour much more than the damage was worth because my mother was scared shitless that I'd be sent to jail."

The poor rich young man who had been raised in wealth without personal restraints was the product of that environment. However Brenda knew that a dangerous element in the boy's personality had to be brought out and fully aired which meant that it would be a long battle for him to change course. "So, are you willing to work at improving yourself?"

"Sure; I want to get out of here."

"Then you are keeping up with your online studies?"

"I'm sure you checked, so you know I do."

Sutton made his way to the offices of Mercer Davis Carroll and Castle, and asked to speak with Cecilia, Castle's assistant. Meeting the detective at the reception, she took him back to her late boss's office and closed the door. A couple of boxes in the corner of the room must have been filled by Malcolm with his dad's belongings, Sutton mused. The walls were now all bare and there was nothing on the desk but the phone.

"How can I help you, detective?" she asked once they were both seated.

"When Mr. Castle worked in his office, did he ever take his jacket off/"

"Most of the time when he wasn't meeting a client. He'd put his jacket over the back of the chair where you're seated."

"So, when he needed to walk around the office, he was in shirt sleeves?"

"Yes. All the lawyers here do that."

"So his jacket was unattended?"

"Sorry?"

"Never mind. Now, I'd like to know when and how often Mr. Lacrosse came into this office to see your boss."

"Quite often. Mr. Lacrosse required a lot of Mr. Castle's time."

"When was the last time he came in here?"

" Last week. No the week before. On the Tuesday."

"How did that go?"

"The door was closed so I couldn't hear what was being said but they did yell at each other for some time, then Mr. Lacrosse stormed out."

"Did Mr. Castle tell you anything about what they discussed?"

She hesitated. "Yes and no. Mr. Castle just said that he wasn't going to be bullied by the likes of Lacrosse."

"He didn't say why he was being bullied?"

"No. But I know he talked to his wife on the phone for a long time after that."

"Well, thank you very much. What are you going to do now? I mean you no longer have a boss."

"Oh I do. I've been asked to work for another lawyer whose assistant is going on maternity leave."

Sutton wished her well, then asked her a favour. "Do you have photos of all the firm's lawyers in your computer?"

"Sure."

"Could you send them to my phone?"

"Of course. No problem."

CHAPTER TWELVE

Detectives Walters and Sutton finalized their research into the history of the partners at Mercer Davis Carroll and Castle.

The firm originally began as Mercer and Mercer, the husband and wife team who struck out on their own after short stints as rookies in large firms. Other lawyers began to join the firm. One of the first one being Arthur Davis who became a partner. After June Mercer left to join a firm of female lawyers devoted solely to female clients Constance Carroll joined the firm. Eventually she was invited to be a partner and was followed a few years later by Murray Castle. As far as the research revealed, there was never any problems between the partners or the associates. Everyone got along.

Gabriel Mercer had been married to June for over thirty-five years, and they had two daughters, both living in the Toronto area. The older one, an editor for a book publisher, worked from home and was married to a commercial airline pilot. They had two boys. The couple hit a bit of a financial rough spot during the pandemic when so many flights were grounded, but they seemed to be getting back on track. The younger one, an accountant with a large firm, had been divorced for a few years and had no children. She had survived the pandemic by working from home and continued to do so as much as she could. The Mercers had been involved for decades in a variety of community groups providing funds to help the underprivileged.

Arthur Davis had been married to his wife, Pamela, for twenty-five years. The second marriage for both. Neither had children with their first partners, but now had a son who was in medical school and living with a nurse. Again no record of any problems, not even parking tickets. Davis and his wife were also involved in the community which, Sutton mused, was a PR effort that helped keep the name of the firm front and center in the Toronto area.

As for Constance Carroll, she and her husband, a judge of the Ontario Superior Court by the name of Harold Evers, had no children. They had been married for more than twenty-five years and were actively involved with financing summer camps for underprivileged children in Ontario.

Sutton caught up with Joey Lacrosse at the jobsite for a new condo building in the north end of Toronto. The man was far from pleased to be accosted by a detective.

"What exactly do you want to know, detective?" Lacrosse barked. "Castle had a heart attack. There's nothing to be investigated."

"We need to know what you and Murray Castle discussed in his office on Tuesday of last week?"

"Why are you wasting my time? Castle is dead. What difference does it make?"

"We are investigating to make sure there was no extenuating circumstances—"

"What circumstances? The guy had a bad heart. Why's the police..." After a moment of silence Lacrosse continued: "Oh, I see. Mercer's now trying to dig up some dirt or scare me so they can get out from under my lawsuit. I bet that's it. Well, it won't work. What Murray and I discussed in his office was something ... something ... it had nothing to do with business or the lawsuit or anything like that. Take my word for it."

"Anything to do with his wife?" Josh Sutton asked.

Looking at the detective, Lacrosse remained silent for a long moment, then said: "I've got to go back to work." With these words he simply walked away.

Detective Sutton looked at the tall Lacrosse go certain that the mention of Brenda Castle had hit a nerve which had sparked in the developer's eyes for half a beat. The man was obviously very adept at managing any physical signs of emotions, but Sutton had detected surprise. Surprise at the mention of the name or surprise that Sutton knew about whatever his relationship with Brenda Castle was?

While trying to assess what he knew for certain and what he could only surmise, Sutton made his way back to the mental hospital. He was hoping to be able to talk to Brenda Castle and he was not disappointed. Her white car was in the parking lot.

Sutton was inquiring at the front counter when he saw Dr. Castle emerge from a door leading to the east wing. She recognized him immediately.

"Detective. Did your investigation of my husband's death lead you here?"

"No, but I would like a few moments of your time if you could."

She hesitated for a moment before saying: "Why not. Let's go into the little parlour."

He followed her through the door to the east wing, an area he was entering for the first time, and he saw a long corridor with many doors on both sides. Brenda Castle opened a door on the right and he followed into what he saw as a small living room with a sofa and some comfortable armchairs. She sat in one of the chairs and he sat across from her.

"What brings you to this neck of the woods, detective?"

"Nothing to do with your husband, I assure you. However running into you gives me a chance to ask you something." She waited. "What is your relationship with Joey Lacrosse?"

The dark eyes burned into his for a moment. The question had come out of left field and he was certain she had never expected that it would ever be asked. However, the most telling was that a relationship of some sort between the two had been confirmed.

"You think I was having an affair with Lacrosse? You've got to be out of your mind."

"Then, tell me why he was bullying your husband?"

She hesitated for the better part of a minute. Sutton waited patiently because he could feel that what she revealed would be most important to his investigation.

She stood and went to the window, staring at a large maple in the back yard. The leaves on it were still in the process of reaching their full size. Suddenly, she said: "Murray was bothered by an allergy at this time of year ... when leaves are coming out. But you know that already."

"Yes, I do."

She turned back to face Sutton. "That's why you took the vitamin bottles from the house. Did you find anything unsafe?"

"Not with the vitamins, but we did find microscopic traces of aconite in the pillbox your husband carried in the inside pocket of his jacket. That indicates that a pill containing the poison was present in the pillbox at some point."

"You think Murray took a poisoned pill thinking it was vitamin?"

" That's exactly what happened."

"And I suppose you think I somehow prepared that poisoned pill?" she said as she sat down again.

"Did you? Or did you pay someone to do it for you?"

"Of course not," she nearly yelled. "I loved Murray. And it certainly was not either of the kids. They adored their father."

"No doubt. But let's back up a little. You didn't tell me why Lacrosse was trying to bully your husband."

"Okay," she finally said after another pause. "He wanted Murray to make sure a certain conclusion, shall we say, would be in my report regarding a patient currently in this hospital. A relative of Lacrosse. In exchange he would cancel the lawsuit against my husband."

"And your husband said no?"

"Murray and I talked about it for a long time, but I could not consent to have my findings influenced by the like of Joey Lacrosse. I know Murray was supposed to meet Lacrosse the day after he died, so I don't think he gave him an answer."

"Do you believe Lacrosse could have murdered Murray over this? To make sure you got the message of the importance of his request?" She remained silent. "That's why you were crying so hard when I first saw you, isn't it? You thought that you were somehow responsible for your husband's death."

She sighed loudly. "I didn't know Murray had been murdered, but I feared the worse. I mean that I could have been the cause of Murray's heart attack."

"Obviously you were not. But could Lacrosse have killed your husband over this?"

"No. Definitely no. Joey's a bully, not a murderer."

Ross Walters had been busy looking into Murray Castle's laptop for more than an hour. So far all he had found in the history listings was research into various businesses, most of them local, as well as into some Ontario lawyers. There was nothing remotely suspicious as far as the detective could deduce. The lawyer had simply been doing searches in the course of helping clients and their businesses.

Walters found the work tiring and looked at his watch. His shift was now over so he decided it was more than time to go home and change for his date with a new woman in his life.

CHAPTER THIRTEEN

Detectives Josh Sutton and Ross Walters parked their sedan and made their way on foot along Spadina in the West Chinatown section of the city, an area which testified to the healthy immigrant population in Toronto. Even if it was relatively early in the day, the place was busy with older East Asians shopping for groceries, outside and inside the stores, and university students on their way to class at the nearby universities looking for fruit and pastries for a quick breakfast

The detectives were enjoying the unique atmosphere in the distinctive neighbourhood. And while specifically looking for shops catering to those who believed in Asian medicine, the two detectives took in the special appeal of the shops packed with all sorts of treasures and distinct garments as well as the many restaurants, from small one-row-of-chairs-around-a-counter types to the more spacious traditional restaurants.

After a while, they turned into a busy side street and almost immediately saw a shop advertising herbal remedies in English and in Chinese symbols, or so they believed. A small bell pealed as they walked in. For the two detectives it was like stepping into a totally different world. An aging Asian man was standing behind a long counter in front of a massive display of all manner of herbs and odd-looking roots and mushrooms in large glass containers on numerous shelves. It was a somewhat impressive and overwhelming display.

"Can I help you?" the man asked in a strongly Chinese-accented voice.

"Yes," Sutton said having decided that the direct approach was the best way to get answers. "We would like to know if you have some aconite in your display here?"

"Very dangerous," the man stated. "Why you want it?"

"I heard it's good for pain."

"Yes, but only for Chinese people. You not Chinese."

"But you do prepare it?"

"Sometimes."

"Can you prepare it so it looks like a pill?"

The man looked at both detectives in turn. Finally he said: "Sorry. No. Want something else?"

"No, thank you," Sutton said, and the two detectives walked out.

"Shouldn't we have probed more?" Walters asked once they were back on the sidewalk.

"Let's face it," Sutton commented, "We may wear suits but it's clear that we have the police look. If he did prepare the pill he was not about to admit it to us. One thing is sure: he's very careful and I think he's too careful to provide any information. We need to investigate in another area. I got one of his cards so we can always call him if needed," Sutton said, putting it in his pocket.

Back at the division office while Sutton was busy researching other herbalists, Ross Walters was back in front of Castle's laptop. He had a coffee nearby and was poised for a boring hour or so before needing to turn his attention to other cases. A few clicks and suddenly he saw that Castle had registered and paid to gain access to a child porn website. After following the steps Castle had used to access the site Walters saw that access was now barred.

He moved to his office computer with its specific capabilities, and soon found out that a UK Paedophile On Line Investigation Team (POLIT) was investigating the people who ran virtual UK-based private networks on the dark web. These networks made it possible for visitors from around the world to share sexually explicit photos and videos of children.

A few more clicks and Walters was chatting with a British law officer who, after Walters provided the proper identification, let him see what the site was all about. The detective nearly fell off his chair. In front of him were rows of photos of children in a variety of abusive poses that indicated more than disrespect for the young, they showed the immorality of men.

He almost screamed as he saw some girls about the age of his ten-year-old twin nieces. Murray Castle had been a degenerate, and for a second Walters considered that his murder had been indeed justified, at least surely in the minds of the parents of those poor children.

POLIT had seized the hard drives of some private networks based on the fact that they were classified as indecent. Law officers were now looking at the people who had spent time on the site Castle had accessed. These networks were paid by credit cards so they had the proper identifications of the visitors however they were adept at scrambling the information.

Walters shared details of the murder of Murray Castle to his overseas contact who then told him that so far they knew of two men in Toronto who regularly visited that particular site. Investigators had dismissed Castle because he had landed on the site only once, using his real name and he had not studied the site nor did he chat with other child porn aficionados like other visitors all did. But the man added that their digital forensic examiners could only do so much and go so far.

Walters was also told that those who accessed child porn sites through private networks were in fact looking for worldwide like-minded groups. Other paedophiles who did not want to be identified by the private network route used library computers where they could remain anonymous. In fact, the British man said there was a very regular visitor who had been identified by his member number as he went around town using Toronto library branches to reach the site.

"You might be in a position to help us there," the man in London said. "Perhaps your local libraries could identify the man since he would have had to be a member and show his membership card." He added that he would forward a listing of the days and time the man went on line in the libraries.

Walters promised that he would investigate and get back to him.

Studying Castle's access to the site Walters saw that the lawyer had gone to the site once just over a month earlier with no indication of repeated visits. He considered that a visitor to a child porn site would have wanted to go back and back again for his personal demented pleasure. Could Castle have been doing research for a case? It certainly did not fit into the kind of law he practiced, however Walters' experience had taught him that the answers to solving crimes were sometimes found at the end of a heretofore unexplored road.

A new direction for the investigation had popped up, but where would it lead?

Walters was anxious to share his findings with Josh Sutton who was on the phone. While he waited he made an effort to calm himself. He knew these types of sites existed and that paedophilia had strong roots in some segments of society, including priests of the Catholic Church, but since he had not yet had to investigate this type of indecent and disgusting behaviour it proved to be a shock. Walters was dedicating his life to keeping the world safe from all manner of criminal activity and he firmly believed that society had the responsibility of making a special effort to protect its children.

How could evil men not abide by that principle choosing instead to destroy the hope and lives of innocent children?

CHAPTER FOURTEEN

Detective Josh Sutton could only agree that his colleague had definitely unearthed a most interesting avenue of investigation. Murray Castle had accessed the porn site for a reason. As far as his assistant was concerned, Castle was not someone who arranged his life around his computer. To him it was simply a tool for information gathering.

Ross Walters had downloaded the information forwarded from London showing details of the days and times a man in Toronto accessed the site using computers in the Toronto libraries. Surely that man was someone Castle knew, otherwise why would he have taken a peak at the sordid website.

But there was no way of knowing the relationship between the two men. Could it be Joey Lacrosse? Perhaps not, Sutton deduced, because he was bullying Castle, not the other way around.

But how would Castle have fought back?

If Castle was threatening to expose the culprit, whomever it was, it could very well have been a motive for murder.

What about other lawyers in his office? Sutton and Walters had a list of the names but not the monikers used to access the child porn site. And what about Gabriel Mercer, Sutton asked Walters, not expecting an answer. Had Castle unearthed his or the other partners' dirty secret?

. . .

There were some 100 branches of the Toronto Library, but the two detectives directed their investigation to the branches where the man identified in London had accessed the site. They began by driving to the closest branch to their location: the North York Central Library. It was part of the history that was Yonge street, an artery that ran from Lake Ontario straight north for the next fifty-six kilometres. The branch was distinguished by the huge cone over the entrance area.

The detectives met with the head librarian in a private room and explained the purpose of their investigation. They had a list of all the personnel employed at the law office of Mercer Davis Carroll and Castle, and needed to check the names against the branch's member-ship data. The librarian called for one of the employees and instructed her to find the information Sutton and Walters needed. The woman was around forty, probably volunteering at the library, Walters assumed, because of comments from his sister about housewives who, like her, enjoyed spending time helping out in libraries. Would she be able to help them?

She was very efficient, and the research was quick and resulted in exactly no match. The detectives asked the woman if she would be able to identify a man, possibly older, who came in pretty regularly to use one of their computers.

"We have a lot of older gentlemen who come in to use our comput-ers," the woman replied. "They want to improve their skills."

Sutton explained. "We're not looking for a retiree, but rather a middle-aged man, no doubt very well dressed. He'd come in at midday or in the evening."

The woman looked puzzled. "You don't have a name?"

"Afraid not. We think he joined your library under an assumed name."

"That would be almost impossible because we require some proof of residence before issuing a library card."

"We believe that he'd have used someone else's information."

She thought for a moment. "Then, I don't see ..."

"Why don't we do it this way," Sutton invited. Using his phone he showed her, one after the other, the pictures of the lawyers in Castle's firm he had gotten from Cecilia. After looking at each one the woman shook her head.

"But you've got to understand that I may not be the best person to identify anyone. I'm here only part time. And never in the evening."

Sutton and Walters talked to other employees who manned the desk where the man would have had to show his library card. None seemed to recall anyone in particular. Sutton left his information card and asked them to call if they remembered something or if they saw someone who might interest the police.

The detectives then traveled to another branch used by the child porn visitor: the Brentwood branch, distinguished by its many large windows, in the borough of Etobicoke. Again none of the employees of the law firm was a member of the branch according to membership records. Questioning the staff in the same way they had done at the previous library did not yield any information.

Sutton nevertheless left his card in the hope that the alert might result in the library personnel being more prone to keep their eyes open.

Sutton and Walters then drove out further afield to the Scarborough Civic Centre in Toronto's eastern borough. The eye-catching building housed one of the city's libraries which, like the other two they had visited, was quite large. People of all ages were either reading newspapers and magazines or working on their own laptops or using the library's desktop units.

Sutton approached the lending desk and asked to speak to the head librarian.

"Sorry, she's not in today. Can I help you with something?" one of the two staff members manning the desk, a tall twenty-something woman asked.

Both detectives showed their badges. Sutton said they wanted to consult the membership data to see if the person they were looking for used the library. After a quick search the woman confirmed that none of their names was listed as a library member.

Sutton pressed the woman to see if she remembered a man who came in to use one of the library's computers and might be using a false name. He proceeded to show the pictures of the lawyers of Castle's firm on his phone. The woman looked at each of them then shook her head.

"The man we are looking for would come in at lunch time or in the evening. Are you here in the evening?"

"I usually work in the evening. Today is an exception."

"What sort of people come into the library in the evening to use the computers?" Walters asked.

"Hum. Well, we get a lot of students and then some regular people who probably don't have internet access at home or because others use the family computer."

Sutton pried some more. "So if a well dressed man came in more or less regularly, you'd remember him, wouldn't you?"

"Huh. Now that you mention it ... there's a fellow who used to come in often but I haven't seen him lately. I remember him because of his shoes."

"Shoes?"

"Well, my father used to own a shoe store, high end brands, and I worked there, but he lost it during the pandemic..."

"Sorry to hear it," Sutton put in. "But what do shoes have to do with the man you remember?"

"Well, I notice shoes when people come in. Force of habit, I suppose. This man wore very expensive shoes."

"You mean sports shoes."

"No. Always primo leather, which made me wonder why he came into the library to use our computers. If he could buy six-hundred-dollar shoes, then he certainly could afford an internet connection at his house."

"What did he look like?"

"Well, he was a bit taller than me. He had a big moustache with gray in it like in his dark hair. And he wore glasses with the heavy black frames like was the style a couple years back."

"How tall was he?" Sutton asked.

"Well, I'm just shy of six feet and I'd say he was about two inches taller."

"He wasn't like six-six, for example?"

"No. I'm sure. Like I said, probably six-two."

"How old would you say he was?"

"I'm not good at guessing ages. He was old. Maybe fifty."

The detectives exchanged a quick look.

Sutton checked his list of dates when the child porn viewers would have been in the library. "If I give you a date when the man would have come in here could you check if a name fits the man you described?

You do have that information don't you? I mean people have to reserve the computers, don't they?"

"Yes, they do. Let me see what I can find."

Sutton gave her a date months earlier, and the woman checked the list of members who had used library computers at seven that evening. "There were three. A woman. I know she is an older person. Then a young guy, probably a student, who comes in all the time. Still does. The third person is a man by the name of Henry Fisher. Is that the person you are looking for?"

"It is now. Do you have an address for him?"

Her fingers got busy on the keyboard. As she rattled off the address and the phone number in the records, Walters wrote it all down.

The detectives thanked the young woman profusely and asked her to call is she happened to remember anything else. They had found their man. The only trouble was that he used a disguise and that he would not be back in the library now that the site he coveted had been shut down. The two men knew that the information he gave the library was certainly false.

Sutton's phone rang and he saw it was the hospital.

CHAPTER FIFTEEN

Dr. Maxwell invited Josh Sutton into his office with a wide sweep of his hand.

"I regret taking you away from your work," the psychiatrist offered.

"My shift was ending so it's all good. How bad was it?" the detective asked.

"It's the breakthrough we were looking for. She finally admitted that little Bryan was gone and would not be back. However, she immediately broke down. I won't lie to you; it was quite traumatic for her to come to terms with reality. I saw the need to sedate her, but I was hoping that you could be here when she wakes up because it's going to be tough."

"I appreciate that, doctor."

The psychiatrist accompanied the detective to Anna's room. They walked in silently to find her asleep.

"How long before she wakes up?" Sutton asked in a whisper.

"Shouldn't be too long. I need to leave but nurse Greta is on duty and will be there for you both."

"Thanks," Josh said as Dr. Maxwell nodded before leaving quietly.

Josh was looking at Anna sleep. With her high cheekbones and dewy skin she was indeed a beautiful woman. At the moment she looked so very peaceful, so totally free of worries and problems. He wondered if the worst was over or if it was the beginning of another hellish period in their lives when he heard a soft knock.

The door opened silently and Greta appeared. "Detective, how are you feeling? About today's breakthrough, I mean?" she whispered.

"I know it must have been so very painful for her, but I'm glad she was well supported."

"Now it can only go better for both of you," she said attempting a smile. "I'm around if you want to talk, need help or anything else. Just push the red button on the wall."

"Thank you, Greta, I appreciate all you're doing for Anna."

"Not especially difficult. She's such a lovely soul." She added: "I'll leave you to your thoughts," and stepped out noiselessly.

Josh stood and went to look out the window which faced the front of the building. He had been rattled when it became clear that paedophilia had somehow been involved in the murder of Murray Castle. While deep down he hoped the investigation would progress into another direction he certainly would do everything in his power to bring the paedophiles to justice. He was incredibly motivated because simply thinking about how children continue to be abused by evil men turned his stomach. He had dearly loved his son and had shed many tears because of his inability to protect and save him when the pandemic saw fit to target such a lovely promising young boy. That reality made him want to scream at the thought that other men, perhaps even fathers, were unable to be awed by the innocence and love of children, and chose instead to wound and damage them.

Was it a mental disease or the work of the devil?

Suddenly he saw a white sedan come in through the two entrance pillars and park. In a moment, Dr. Brenda Castle was getting out of the car and making her way to the front door. What was she doing at the hospital at that time of day, Josh wondered . And it wasn't Monday. None of his concern, he admitted to himself.

He went back to sit near his wife, trying to divine their future. Was there hope that Anna would not relapse into periods of avoidance when faced with any other of life's difficult episodes? That was certainly a concern if they were to have another child. That suggestion from Anna had been on his mind as he thought about the possibility of them starting over as a new family.

Anna stirred. Slowly she opened her eyes and looked at her husband with eyes that seemed lost.

"Hi, honey. How are you feeling?" he asked.

She did not reply and closed her eyes. Several minutes passed before she opened them again and made an effort to smile at him.

"Hi. How are you feeling?" he asked again.

"I guess Dr. Maxwell told you about today?"

"Yes, he did. How do you feel now?"

"Okay. At least as well as can be," she said then her eyes filled with tears. "It's hard to accept that our darling Bryan is gone."

Taking her hand into his, he said: "I know, honey. But don't you think of him as a little angel up there helping us go on?"

"That's a nice thought," she said among her tears. "I want to go home."

"I know. We'll talk to Dr. Maxwell tomorrow and get his input, okay?"

"Okay."

There was a soft knock at the door and Greta appeared with a dinner tray. "Hi, Anna. How are you feeling?"

"Good now that Josh is here."

The nurse deposited the tray on the bed table. "Want to eat in bed, or would you prefer the chair?"

"The chair. The chair." She sat up, pulled herself to her feet and Josh held her hand as she sat in an easy chair. Greta lowered the table, pulled it over Anna's knees and removed the cover over a plate. "Chicken pot pie," Greta said in a proud voice.

"My favourite," Anna exclaimed.

Greta smiled before leaving. She was soon back with a second tray. "Some dinner for you, detective," she said. "Can't have our Anna eating alone, can we?" She deposited his tray on the table in front of the window.

"You are so very kind. Thank you."

"Enjoy," she said and left.

The tasty meal was a favourite of both of them which made Josh question for a quick moment the serendipity of it. He quickly turned his attention to Anna and they talked about his work, the weather, her mother, and anything else that avoided the elephant in the room. As they were ending the meal with their coffee, Anna said: "I'm sorry, Josh, for causing you so much trouble."

"You've got nothing to be sorry for. You reacted to a severe traumatic loss the only way you knew how. That's it."

She smiled at him and he saw in her eyes the connection they had often shared in their ten years together. He smiled back. Could life be back on track at long last? He hoped so with all his being.

Reluctantly, when Anna's eyes seemed to be closing as they talked, Josh saw the wisdom of letting her rest after a very eventful day. He guided her to bed and kissed her good night. She was asleep before he made it to the door.

As he was going down the staircase leading to the reception area he saw Brenda Castle in what seemed like an intense discussion with Joey Lacrosse. He stopped half way down. Their voices were low so he couldn't make out everything that was said, but soon Dr. Castle's voice got louder as she said: "No. And that's final."

Lacrosse was put out. "You may regret this, doctor."

"What are you going to do? Bully me like you bullied Murray?"

Without replying, he turned on his heels and left through the front door.

Josh continued down, and the psychologist saw him.

"Detective, you're here again."

"Visiting a relative. May I ask if Lacrosse is threatening you?"

"I can take care of myself."

"I'm sure you can, but you could ask for a restraining order."

"I know, but that could make matters worse."

"Again, if he's threatening you, we can take steps ..."

"I know you want to help, but please leave it alone," she said before disappearing through a side door.

CHAPTER SIXTEEN

The next morning Walters reported what was expected. The address Mr. Henry Fisher had given the library did not exist. The street off The Danforth did exist but not the number. As for the phone number it was the main number for the Toronto City Hall. As for giving proof of residence to the library it was only a matter of presenting a copy of a credit card bill where the name and address would have been modified. Easy to do these days with everything computers can execute, the detective concluded. As for not presenting a driver's license he could easily have said that he had lost it and that it would be a few days before he got a new one.

With that information, Josh Sutton was giving a review of the investigation into Murray Castle's murder to captain Corbett.

"While we know, more or less, who probably killed Castle it'd be impossible to look into all the herbalists in Toronto in an attempt to find out which one prepared the deadly pill. It had to have been prepared by a specialist because certainly none of the people close to Castle would have known how. I figure the specialist was paid very well to keep his mouth shut. Or perhaps the killer had something on the specialist. It's all rather complicated and secretive. A quiet murder with no physical evidence of any sort. A regular murder where you can examine the weapon, the fingerprints and the DNA, and talk to witnesses, is louder and easier."

Corbett chuckled. "I like your analogy. No doubt it's the type of murder we don't see every day, but if you and Ross continue to dig at it, you're bound to find something."

"Yeah, I'm sure we will. In time. By the way, captain, Anna is doing a lot better. She has finally been able to talk about Bryan with her therapist."

"That's great news, Josh. Is there anything I can do?"

Josh shook his head. "Not now, but thanks. Her psychiatrist will keep me apprised of her progress. Hopefully she'll be able to come home soon."

"Well, good luck. And keep me informed about the case and your wife."

Back in his own work area, Sutton knew he had to keep busy to avoid going bonkers thinking about Anna. He called Brenda Castle. She answered on the second ring.

"Dr. Castle, this is detective Sutton—"

"Oh. I saw it was a call from the police but I certainly did not expect it'd be you."

"You were not surprised to get a call from the police? May I ask why?"

"I work with the Toronto police from time to time. An officer calls when they want me to come down to a division and talk to a suspect to quickly assess their mental health, their mental capacity."

"I see. My reason for calling is that I want to discuss the investigation into your husband's murder with the benefit of your professional expertise. When would you be free?"

"So I take it you no longer consider me a suspect!"

"I don't believe we ever seriously considered that you murdered your husband. What I want to talk about are some personality aspects of the person we believe killed your husband."

"You know who it is? Someone I know?"

"You'll have to tell us."

They met in a gazebo in a large park a short distance from the Castle home. She looked very relaxed in a pair of jeans and a bulky white sweater. The warming weather was perfect for enjoying the spring air.

The sun was shining in a perfect azure sky in its descent toward the horizon, and the birds were paying tribute to it all with their melodious sounds.

"So, what exactly are you looking for," Brenda asked once they were both at ease on the bench that lined the inside railing of the structure.

"As I told you, we now know that someone killed your husband by putting a poisonous pill that looked like the vitamin C pills he carried in the little pillbox in the inside pocket of his jacket. We have determined that it was done at his office although we can't know when. I mean we don't know if it was the day your husband died or a previous day.

"Now we believe the poison was put in the pillbox at the office because your husband would take off his jacket when he was working and drape it on the back of one of his chairs. We believe that the tablet was put inside the pillbox while he was away from his office walking around in his shirt sleeves. It was the perfect opportunity. The amazing thing is that it could have been done at any time, any day. The killer himself could have done it or he could have paid or forced an employee to do it.

"We have also determined the motive. Some months ago your husband visited a child porn site—"

"What? You must be mistaken. Murray was certainly not that kind of man," Castle almost screamed.

"Don't worry. We know he was not. He visited the site just once, and we believe it was simply for research. We have determined that he probably found out, by accident or otherwise, that someone close to him spent time on child porn sites. Your husband probably confronted the man in the hope of making him stop, of helping him. We believe that the man, fearing his vice might become common knowledge decided that the best way out of this dilemma was to kill your husband to silence him.

"Of course, the killer was banking on the fact that there would not be an autopsy," Sutton concluded. "The fact that there was one must have affected his psyche."

"I take it you have no idea who the man in question is?"

"We know he accessed the site at a library using a false name and a disguise. That's where we are right now."

"Amazing," Castle commented.

"Are we to assume that your husband never told you about having discovered that someone he knew visited child porn sites?"

"Murray seldom talked about the details of his work, but now I know why he had become distant, preoccupied. He was not having an affair."

"You say your husband didn't discuss his work with you, but he did discuss Joey Lacrosse with you, did he not?"

"That was different because it concerned me."

"And the man is now trying to influence a report you have to prepare, correct?"

She did not react.

Sutton continued. "We know your husband's killer hired someone to prepare the poisoned pill. We don't yet know who."

"You believe it might be Lacrosse? Lacrosse is a bully, a scared boy who needs to attack people before they attack him. He's not the killer type. He's the 'scare them' type."

"May I inquire about the nature of his request to your husband?"

"You may ask ... Okay, the young man I need to evaluate who is in Montrose at the moment is Joey's nephew, the son of his sister. She wants me to say that he's totally non-violent when that's not the case. At least not at this point in time. She asked Joey to convince me to go along with her wishes, Joey approached Murray."

"When is your evaluation expected?"

"Two weeks from now. Don't worry. I won't let Joey derail me"

"Good. Now about the killer. What kind of personality would dream up such an elaborate murder scenario?"

"Very attentive to details, for one thing. Like lawyers are, I must say. Also, I think this was very personal, in the sense that it was survival for the killer. He could not accept Murray urging him to get help, to see the error of his ways, as it were. Because that's what my poor husband would have done. He was not perfect, but Murray always tried to help people, to make the world a better place."

"So, do you believe it could be one of the partners in your husband's firm? You know them all pretty well, don't you?"

"I do, but their work means they stand for justice, for what is right, so I don't see any of them as murderers. Of course, people can kill when they feel trapped in what they judge as a serious situation from which they don't see any escape."

"In this case, the culprit was no doubt fearful that your husband would expose him in front of his peers, indeed the whole Ontario judicial structure, as a degenerate pervert. That could have lead to his deciding that your husband was a liability and that he needed to be eliminated. Do you agree?"

"Very possible, but so terribly sad. I wish Murray would have discussed the matter with me. Examining the problem together we might have been able to come up with a solution that would have saved his life," Dr. Castle concluded sadly.

Josh Sutton felt sorry for the psychologist who might very well feel that there should have been more communication in their marriage.

CHAPTER SEVENTEEN

Sutton went alone to the residence of Constance Carroll, a unit in a luxurious condo building west of the Yorkdale district. He considered that it was probably chosen because it was an easy drive to any part of the city, even Pearson airport. As a lawyer, she probably had to move around the city from time to time, and he considered that this location was perfect.

He had decided on a cold call. In the lobby, he rang the unit on the tenth floor. A woman's voice was heard: "Yes?"

She was looking at Sutton who was standing in front of the camera relaying a view of the space just inside the door.

"Mrs. Carroll, I'm detective Sutton of the Toronto police, and I need to talk to you."

"What is it about?"

"I will explain when we talk," Sutton replied.

"Does it have to be now?"

"Afraid so. Yes."

"You should have called. I need a minute to get dressed. You can come up and wait by the door to the unit."

"Fine," Sutton said.

The unlocking buzzer made it possible for him to step inside. He saw that the foyer extended to a parlour-type room decorated with some exotic plants that accented the easy chairs in a matching rich grey tint. He assumed the building was relatively new, and took the elevator for ten stories. He found the unit number and waited as requested. A minute later the door opened and Sutton was taken aback by the many bruises that decorated the face of the slim woman in front of him who was wearing jeans and a white tee. Her face was obviously swollen. She invited him in.

"Now you know," was her first words.

"Ma'am?"

"By your reaction, I take it you didn't know I had facial surgery—a facelift. We all want to look younger than we are, don't we?" she asked no one in particular. "I often have to argue cases in court where appearance is important." She frowned briefly. "Why are you here, detective?"

"You are aware, I take it, of the death of your partner Murray Castle."

"Of course. The poor man!"

From the photos online he had put her at mid-fifties, perhaps older. She had obviously been trying to remove some of those years from her face.

She invited him to sit in the living room where the rug and most of the furniture was white. He took an easy chair and she sat on a love seat accented with colourful pillows. He judged that the art on the walls was pricey, like the one in the law firm office. Among the photographs on the baby grand was one of Constance with a man who appeared only slightly older than her. Although he was not certain, Sutton assumed that the man was Constance Carroll's husband. He met so many people in the course of investigations.

"How long had you known Murray Castle?"

"Well, ever since he joined the firm as a rookie. I myself didn't have that many years of experience at that time, so we both sort of grew up together as lawyers."

"Was there ever any tension between the two of you?"

"Why are you asking me all these questions? Murray had a heart attack, so there's no reason to investigate anything."

"Ma'am, Murray Castle was murdered. He was poisoned. That caused the heart attack."

"That can't be. Murray was a great guy."

"So everybody says."

Sutton was surprised by her calmness. Usually women reacted to murder, whether they knew the person or not. "Didn't your partners tell you that it was a homicide?"

"Because of my surgery no one has called for fear of disturbing me I suppose, so I didn't get any details. And I haven't been keeping up with the news. How was he poisoned?"

"Someone put a pill laced with poison with his vitamins."

It was difficult to tell if her face showed any emotionality. It was too bruised and swollen.

"Well, I didn't do it," she stated clearly.

"We have to investigate everyone who was close to him."

"I understand. Any other questions?"

"You left your office the day Castle died?"

"That's right. I left as I had planned. After they took the body away there was no need for me to stick around. Especially since everybody in the office was quite upset as you can imagine."

"I'm sure. Well, that's it for now. I will get back to you if we need more information." He stood up and pointed to the shiny black baby grand. "Is that your husband in that picture."

"Yes. That's Harold. Harold Evers. He's a judge. A superior court judge."

"Thank you for your time."

Sutton left realizing that he knew curly haired judge Evers because he had testified at a trial two or three years earlier where he was the presiding judge.

Back at the division, Sutton confirmed that Judge Harold Evers had been, for almost a decade, an Ontario superior court judge with an impressive record of law and order. It would follow that his wife would also be a law and order advocate. A power couple seeking justice. While he never dismissed any possible suspects until the culprit had been identified, Sutton did not believe that Constance Carroll could have killed Castle because they knew a man had done it.

But did they?

Also, as far as he knew only one woman in Toronto had ever been charged with paedophilia over the years which was not surprising since the number of females suffering from the disorder and other sexual perversions was considerably minimal compared to male sufferers according to the discussions by experts he had read online.

He dismissed Constance Carroll as a suspect knowing that he needed to look more closely at Castle's two other partners.

CHAPTER EIGHTEEN

Before going home at the end of his work day, Josh Sutton went to have dinner with Anna at the hospital after having a long phone conversation with Dr. Maxwell. The psychiatrist was cautiously optimistic that Anna was well on her way to recovery and told Josh that a few more days would allow her to grieve, a process she was only now starting to experience.

The detective had called Greta to inform her of his plan, and the nurse promised that she would make certain that dinner would be special. He wasn't quite sure what she had meant, but he trusted that she would arrange a nice meal.

He found Anna in her room, still in her yoga outfit, looking out the window. She didn't turn when he called her name. Approaching he saw that she'd been crying.

"It'll be okay, honey," he said, holding her close. "I promise."

"You know you can't promise that."

"Honey, everything will be okay if we're together."

She looked up at him and attempted a smile. "Can I come home now?"

"The doctor says he'd like you to stay just a few more days. You should be able to come home early next week. Maybe your mother could come to be with you during the day for a while to help you settle in. What do you say?"

"If you say so."

"Your mother lost a grandchild, so she's grieving too. It would help her."

She looked out the window again. "You're right. She loved Bryan so much."

"Perhaps you should call her and begin making arrangements."

"I'll talk to her tomorrow."

They both sat and talked about Bryan for a while. He knew that was the way to go so they could reach a point when the good memories would overshadow the tremendous loss. Then they talked about his work. While he never discussed details of his investigations with her or anyone else outside law enforcement, he did tell her that he was working on a case involving lawyers.

"Hope you put them all in jail," she said with some passion.

He chuckled knowing her disdain for lawyers after one of her best friends had lost a case. The woman was suing her ex-husband for assault, but somehow her lawyer who had all the information and details of the attack managed to let the ex get away with it.

Greta knocked lightly and came in with a tray she put down on the bed table. There were two plates and when the nurse removed the domed covers it revealed two bowls of chilli along with salads and crusty bread.

"Wow," Josh exclaimed. "You outdid yourself."

"Our chef is renowned for his chilli. Enjoy."

"Thank you, Greta," Anna said.

"My pleasure, dear."

Josh left the hospital in a more positive mood than usual. The light at the end of the tunnel was now getting closer and closer. How great it was going to be to have his Anna at home to take his mind off his current investigation! He prayed that nothing would stand in the way of it becoming a reality.

While he was certain that everyone has to face the lessons the Universe bestows on everyone, he knew that he and Anna had paid with the life of their son. He mused that, as a lesson, it had been a cruel one, one that still made his soul scream.

As he continued driving Sutton's thoughts turned to the Castle murder. The detectives' earlier searches had found nothing amiss in the lives of Castle's partners. The three seemed to be pillars of the community. However, Sutton knew that appearances can be deceiving, that he and Walters had to dig further. Suddenly his phone buzzed.

He slowed his car to the curb before answering even if he could active it through his ear bud. He did not recognize the number.

"Detective Sutton, this is Karen at the Scarborough library," she said, her voice low. "The man you were looking for, Henry Fisher, is here now."

"I'll be right there," he replied urgently.

Sutton's personal car was equipped with a dash emergency light. He activated it, pulled it up and placed it on the dashboard. He wanted to reach the library as quickly as possible and he needed to clear the road. The light ensured that drivers would see it in their rearview mirrors and, hoping they were not being pulled over, would get out of the way.

He sped to reach a 401 ramp that would take him east to Scarborough. He made it in record time. After parking, he rushed inside the distinctive building. Karen saw him come in.

"So sorry, detective, but he's gone. He left five minutes ago. He was here just ten minutes or so. I saw him leave but I couldn't stop him."

"Appreciate you letting me know. Would you have any way of knowing what websites he might have searched?"

"I looked at the unit he used, but he had deleted his search history."

"Did you see what kind of car he was driving?"

"No. Afraid not."

"What was he wearing?"

"He had on a suit. Looked expensive."

"Anything else?"

"Not that I can think of."

"Thank you for helping our investigation. You'll let us know if he comes in again?"

"Of course. What did he do?"

Sutton saw the wisdom of being vague. "We don't know yet."

The detective drove away from the library disappointed that he had missed his suspect, but he was glad that he now had a mole in the library who would keep an eye out. He was also very pleased that Mr. Fisher clearly did not suspect that he was under scrutiny.

Once home, he left work behind and went around the house looking for things that needed to be done before Anna came home. In the main bedroom, he would change the sheets and put a bit more order in his closet. Hers was as she had left it. Perfectly orderly. The guest bedroom was immaculate, just as it was the day Anna left. No one had used it since.

He opened the door to Bryan's room slowly. Nothing had been touched since the day Anna left, which meant that it was exactly how it was the day the poor little guy had been taken to the hospital. Colourful toys were strewed around the room and the bed was still unmade. Josh thought about washing the sheets, but decided against it. Anna would need to take those steps herself to make peace with the Universe as she resumed her life, now forever changed.

He closed the door and walked to the kitchen in search of a cookie.

CHAPTER NINETEEN

The next morning, Josh Sutton went looking for the police's sketch artist, a young fellow by the name of Pete.

"I need your talent, if you're not too busy."

"I'm at your service, detective. What do you need?"

Sutton brought up the picture of Gabriel Mercer on his phone for Pete to see. "If I send you this pic and another one, can you alter them by adding a moustache and brown hair, both with a good amount of grey. And a pair of black-rimmed glasses."

"Of course. No problem."

"If you could make a couple sketches for each and change the amount of grey in each, that would be a great help."

"I can do that. Things are quiet right now. It'll be fun."

Sutton sent the photos of the two partners Mercer and Davis on his phone to Pete's computer. "Call me when you're done."

Pete promised to let Sutton know as soon as he had something.

At the noon hour, the man who called himself Henry Fisher walked into the Scarborough library to claim his reservation and use one of their computers. Soon he was busy at the unit closest to the back away from other people although none of the other computers were in use at the time.

The man was soon on a child porn site, chatting with other sick individuals bent on hurting innocent children. After less than an hour he cleared his history, turned off the machine and was out the door.

Josh Sutton was ending his workday with paperwork when a light bell announced the arrival of an email. Pete was sending him the sketches he had prepared. The detective was impressed by what he saw. The two law partners were now completely different men. He didn't think that he himself would recognize either of them. As Sutton had requested there were two sketches for each of the men, one with some grey in the moustache and hair, the other with a lot more. He couldn't wait to show them to Karen to get her reaction. She was the key that could guide them to the killer.

When he arrived at the library, Karen smiled at Sutton from behind the lending desk.

"Can you get away for a few moments? I've something to show you."

She said she could and told her fellow workers that she had to step away. Sutton followed her to an empty reading room.

She quickly spoke. "Before you begin, I've got to tell you that Fisher was in earlier, at lunch time, and used a computer for almost one hour. I check every day to see if he came in before my shift begins. Is that any help?"

"Very much. It tells us that he'll be in again."

"I'll keep my eyes open," she said.

Sutton then proceeded to spread the sheets of the four printed sketches on one of the tables in the room.

She looked closely at them then, much to the disappointment of the detective, said that neither was the man who called himself Henry Fisher.

"Are you quite sure?"

"Oh, yes. The man who comes in is more fleshy. I mean he has a double chin. These two guys here are slimmer. Also, the guy's face is rounder." Taking time to sit at one of the chair, she told Sutton that she was sure because she was an artist by day. "The library is not my main job. I do visuals for book covers and children's picture books for a living. Not quite yet a real living because I'm not well known, but I'm getting there. Working here gives me a chance to see the new design

87

trends in publishing." Then as an afterthought she added: "Sorry I'm disappointing you, detective."

Sutton sat down himself, feeling a bit deflated. "Not a problem. Detective work involves lots of misdirection." He then quickly rallied. "Would you then be able to sketch the face of Mr. Fisher for us?"

"I could try. I took a good look at him last time he was in."

"That would be great," Sutton said, and the deal was concluded.

Anna Sutton looked out of her window at the beautiful spring day, and told herself that she had to try to continue to be more positive. A walk in the sunshine in the back garden would help her continue to heal especially if she had someone to walk and chat with.

After her yoga lesson she had changed into a pair of jeans and a tee and was now looking for the beige jacket she especially liked. She put it on and made her way to the nurses' station where she told the nurse on duty that she was going for a walk outside.

"Nice day for it. Good for you."

"I'll be back in twenty minutes," Anna said.

The nurse told her to take her time.

As she was walking down the staircase Anna saw Fran, one of the women in her yoga class, who was dealing with the demons of her childhood because her father had abused her for a long period. The two women talked from time to time each making an effort to clarify their problems in their own minds.

"I'm going for a walk in the garden. Why don't you come with me? It's nice outside," Anna invited.

"Okay. Let me get a jacket. I'll be back in a jiffy."

The two women stepped into a brilliant sunshine and were soon walking on one of the paths that zigzagged around still barren flower beds. They had yet to talk about the issues that kept them in the hospital when Garrett Perkins approached.

"Why you look at me?" he asked.

"What are you talking about?" Fran wanted to know.

Anna spoke. "You're right in front of us. Where else are we going to look?"

The young man was taken aback for a moment but quickly rallied. "I need a smoke. Give me a smoke."

"We don't smoke," Fran said.

"The hospital doesn't allow smoking. You know that," Anna said.

"People here smoke all the time, outside. You came outside to smoke, didn't you?"

"No. We just wanted to walk," Anna said.

"I don't believe you," Perkins said pulling out a knife to emphasize his comment. He got closer to Anna and repeated his request for a smoke.

Suddenly Anna realized that the situation could quickly evolve into a life-threatening one, something she was ill equipped to deal with at the moment, and froze. As Perkins made a threatening gesture with the knife towards Anna, Fran began screaming at the top of her lungs. It made Perkins nervous and before Anna could move away he stabbed her in a shoulder. Blood quickly darkened her beige jacket and Perkins immediately hit her again, this time in the arm, then ran away as guards rushed to the scene.

CHAPTER TWENTY

As he was entering his division, Sutton's phone buzzed. He saw that Dr. Maxwell was calling. He answered with apprehension.

"Detective, can you come over as quickly as possible? It's very important."

"What's the problem?"

"Let's talk about it when you get here," and hung up.

Sutton told Walters he would be away for a while because of Anna and to let the captain know, then rushed out the door.

He drove his own car and thought about using the dash light to make his journey quicker, then dismissed the idea. He was not, after all, out on police business, he was simply an ordinary citizen worried sick about his wife. He wondered if his instincts were kindling the fear at the bottom of his stomach or if he had really detected some anxiety in the calm psychiatrist's voice. Not knowing what was going on was very quickly darkening his thoughts, while he hoped he would not be stopped for speeding as he pressed his foot on the gas pedal ever more firmly.

When he finally reached the hospital, Sutton remained seated in his car for a minute. He had to try to relax. It could be something very minor, but then again it had to be important for the doctor to call in the middle of the day.

As soon as he got to the second floor, nurse Greta met him. "Detective, Dr. Maxwell asked to be informed the minute you got here. Let me do that now," she said pleasantly and made her way to the nurses' station and a phone.

"I'll be in Anna's room," Sutton said.

Greta told him that she wasn't in her room, and that he should wait for Dr. Maxwell.

The psychiatrist appeared less than five minutes later, yet to Sutton it had been an eternity. "Let's go in here," Maxwell invited and Sutton followed him to a small alcove with two chairs for cozy conversations.

After asking the detective to remain calm, the doctor told him the bad news. "I regret to tell you that Anna is in our active medical area at the moment under the care of our on-call physician who has been with her since the incident occurred."

"What kind of incident?"

"She was attacked by one of our patients, but the doctor says she'll be just fine. She's sedated at the moment."

Sutton felt that a bowling ball had hit his stomach. "What kind of attack?"

"A young man here under observation assaulted her with a knife. Luckily, because she was wearing a jacket, the wounds were not very deep."

Sutton wanted to scream. "How in hell could that have happened?"

"Anna and another patient were out walking in the garden at the back taking advantage of the sunshine when the young man asked the two women for a cigarette. Since neither had one it enraged him and he suddenly took out a knife. Your wife's friend screamed but by the time the guards were able to reach them Anna had been stabbed. Fortunately, the injuries are not life threatening by any means. Anna was stabbed in the arm and the shoulder. While the wounds were not deep, there was a lot of blood which horrified her. I suppose it took her back to her worst fears."

"So what you're telling me is that the progress she had made has been nullified?"

"I wouldn't say nullified, more like paused for a period of time."

"Nice! I thought this place was safe," Sutton said in an accusing tone.

"Believe me, it's the first such incident in this hospital. The police were called and they have taken the young man into custody."

"That does not make me feel better, doctor. Was he your patient?"

"No. He's a patient of Dr. Castle."

Josh Sutton was looking at Anna while she slept propped up on the hospital bed with one arm and one shoulder bandaged. She looked so helpless, he thought. Why did she have to be attacked now that they were both looking forward to renewing their lives? He could feel the anger rising in his soul. He would find out to what division the young man was taken and would tell his story to the court to make certain the would-be killer was not released on bond.

Anna stirred and opened her eyes.

"How are you feeling?" he asked.

She spoke after taking a moment to clear the fog in her mind. "I was so scared. I saw his knife but I didn't think he would use it... He looked drunk."

"Drunk or high?"

"One of the two."

"Did he say why he was angry?"

"He thought Fran and I were outside in the yard so we could smoke. He got mad when we couldn't give him a cigarette."

"That's crazy," Sutton said. "Which is exactly what he is. I want to go now so I can make sure he is not released on bail. I'll be back later."

Anna smiled. "I'll be here."

He kissed her and left.

Once outside, Sutton called Walters and explained what had happened at the hospital.

"Can you find out where the guy, name of Garrett Perkins, was taken. I want to go and make sure he's not released."

"Give me a couple minutes."

"I'll wait in my car."

His phone buzzed just over a minute later. "He's at the downtown."

"Thanks. I'm going there and will let you know what happens."

CHAPTER TWENTY-ONE

Sutton rushed into the main division building where he talked to the stern-looking officer on the desk. "I want to see whoever is in charge of the Perkins case. I work at the northwest. My name is Sutton."

"I know who you are, detective. Let me see what I can find out," the officer said as she got busy on the phone.

Sutton looked around and saw that the downtown division was busy as usual. There were some people on the benches against the wall. Two uniformed policemen were talking to one of them. He turned when he heard his name.

"Hi. Come on back and we can chat," the young investigator with a really short haircut, who introduced himself as Porter, invited. He took Sutton to the area where an assortment of law enforcement personnel was fighting Toronto's crime scene. Porter sat at a desk and Sutton took one of the chairs next to it. Sutton made sure the rookie investigator knew about Anna.

"Your wife? So sorry. I saw the name Sutton but didn't make the connection."

"I want to know what Perkins's being charged with?" Sutton asked urgently.

"As it stands with aggravated assault with a weapon."

"You must pump it up to attempted murder."

"You sure that's what you see?"

"Yes, I'm sure. When does he go before a judge?"

"Tomorrow."

"Did you talk to the psychologist who was treating him?"

"Not yet but we have her information."

"His lawyer will try to get him out on bond. This can't happen. If he gets bail he'll return to the hospital and might go after my wife again."

"Doubtful he'll be released. He's a patient at a mental hospital but I'll talk to the crown prosecutor."

Sutton went back to see his Anna. She was watching television and appeared calm, much to his relief.

"Josh, you don't need to worry," she began. "The guy's gone and won't be back. I'm healing."

He bent down and kissed her cheek. "You're a trooper."

"I want to go home as soon as possible. I talked to my mother today and she's excited about being with me for a bit when I'm released."

"Great. Did the doctor say when that could be?"

"He said he'd make a decision tomorrow."

"You will call me when you know."

"Who else would it tell?" she said with a bright smile.

It was almost enough to make up for the scare earlier in the day.

Later Sutton's phone buzzed as he was at his desk and thinking about going home. He did not recognize the number.

"Detective Sutton, this is Karen at the library."

"Oh, hi Karen. You've got something for me?"

"I do. I've done the sketch of Henry Fisher like I remember him. I have your email address on the card you gave me so I could send it right now."

"That'd be great. Thank you so much."

"You know, the more I thought about it when I was working on the sketch, the more I think he had his own hair. I mean, I think the two men you showed me were probably bald, or at least partly bald."

"Boy, you've got a good eye. You are quite right. Both are balding, but how could you tell?"

"When I was studying art, our teacher taught us how to distinguish a rug—a wig—from real hair. I found it fascinating."

"Can I call you back when I get the sketch?"

"Of course."

In less than a minute the picture of a sketch appeared on his phone. Wow, he thought to himself, she's good. Another minute and she was answering the phone.

Sutton could not hide the fact that he was impressed. "Boy, Karen, that's very good."

"Thanks. That's what he looks like."

"I see what you meant when you said he was fleshier than the men I showed you. A much rounder face. You should come work for us as a sketch artist."

She hesitated for a moment. "I think I'll stay with my work."

"Good for you. Again, thank you."

"I'm glad to be able to help. I'm still checking every day to see if the guy's name comes up in the list of reservations for computers, but so far nothing other than the two I told you about already. I'll let you know the next time he does come in."

Sutton thanked her again grateful for modern communications which meant he didn't have to go all the way to the eastern section of the city to look at the sketch even if the rush hour was essentially over by now.

He looked at the sketch again, thinking: I know you from somewhere, you pervert. It'll come to me and I'll catch you.

Progress was slow but steady. He knew he'd solve the case, but not tonight. Now it was time to go home.

The next morning Sutton and Walters were reviewing the Castle case. When looking at the sketch Karen had made Sutton remarked that it reminded him of someone, although he couldn't place who just yet but that it would come to him. The ringing phone on his desk interrupted. He was told that he had a visitor at the front.

When he got there, he was surprised to see Dr. Brenda Castle. He immediately knew that she had slept poorly.

"Can we talk, detective?"

"Certainly. Follow me."

He took her to an interview room in the back and asked her if she could use some coffee. She nodded. He left and returned a few moments later with two filled mugs. She took a sip before speaking.

"I wanted to stop by before going downtown. I have to be on hand when Garrett Perkins goes before the judge. Anyway I came in to say how sorry I am that Garrett attacked your wife."

"It wasn't your fault."

"Of course it was. I knew he had control issues and I should have seen that it went deeper than what was on the surface. I somehow believed that he would behave himself because he told me he couldn't wait to leave Montrose. His parents had insisted that he stay there until I said he was no longer a threat. Of course, I didn't know he had smuggled a knife into the hospital. Orderlies are supposed to check everything patients bring in their luggage and on their bodies when they're admitted. Obviously, they missed the knife. He had no visitors during the short period of time he was at the hospital so no one smuggled it in for him. The hospital will be investigating and make sure it doesn't happen again." She stopped for a sip of coffee, then asked: "How's your wife doing? Will she be okay?"

"Yes. She seems to be recuperating well. Thank you."

"May I ask the reason for her being in the hospital?"

Sutton hesitated, but then quickly considered that his therapist had told him that talking about it to people who were interested in knowing was always a good idea. "She needed help to come to term with the fact that we lost a young son."

"Oh, I'm so sorry for your loss, detective," Castle said, and Sutton could feel the sincerity in her dark eyes.

"Thank you. But she's now very much on the mend. The knife attack's certainly not helping though. I've been thinking of suing the hospital, the young man and his parents. Perhaps even you." Looking straight at her he added: "Regrettably that's the reality."

She was quiet for a long moment. "I can't blame you," she finally said.

"I'll be talking to a lawyer and from there decide how to proceed."

"Again, I am so sorry, detective. You are aware that Garrett is the nephew of Joey Lacrosse."

"Of course. We've talked about that. But outside of the fact that Lacrosse tried to bully you through your husband, as far as I can tell he bears no responsibility for his nephew's attack. Unless he convinced the young man to do something to discredit you."

Castle sat straighter and looked Sutton in the eyes. "You believe it's a possibility?"

"Ma'am, in my line of work I learned a long time ago that anything is possible when it comes to what triggers people and what they are capable of doing."

CHAPTER TWENTY-TWO

When Sutton arrived at the new Toronto court house, he went through security and was allowed to keep his weapon because of his role as a detective. He checked the daily roster and made his way to the courtroom assigned for the bail hearings. Perkins was listed as the last name and would be ending the morning session.

As he entered the courtroom Sutton saw that there were few people in the gallery. Brenda Castle was seated in the first row behind the crown prosecutor, no doubt waiting to testify. Behind the defence lawyer a couple in their fifties who were Perkins' parents, Sutton assumed. A few seats from them sat Joey Lacrosse.

Television shows and movies depicting American courtrooms and lawyers in action were essentially the same as what took place in Canadian courtrooms. Here the difference was that the lawyers wore long black robes with white collar tabs. He knew the tradition had its roots in England, however across the pond English barristers also wore wigs, although only for arguing criminal cases. More than once Sutton had heard Canadian lawyers say that luckily they did not have to wear those heavy ugly white wigs.

Both lawyers were busy reviewing the documents in front of them. The assistant crown prosecutor was a tall gentleman with greying hair. Sutton had seen him in action at one of the trials where he had testified and judged him to be around fifty. At the defence table was a woman in her forties with short black hair, a lawyer he had never seen before.

A side door suddenly opened and nineteen-year-old lanky Garrett Perkins was brought in. He was wearing a dark blue suit and was greeted by his lawyer. Instead of sitting beside her he slouched into the chair. The lawyer said something and Garrett quickly sat properly. Sutton noticed that the accused did not look in the direction of his parents.

In a moment, people were asked to stand as the judge came in and took her seat. She was a short mature woman whose hair was all white and who was probably preparing for retirement by handling an easier load, like bail hearings. After everyone was seated she asked the crown prosecutor to read the charge.

Assistant crown prosecutor Neil Millay stood and read from a prepared text, no doubt written by Porter, the young police investigator. Garrett Perkins had been charged with aggravated assault resulting in bodily injury. He explained that the attack had taken place at a private mental hospital where Perkins was in the process of being evaluated by a psychologist. He added that the knife used in the attack had been smuggled in which clearly meant that the young accused did intent to cause harm.

Sutton was disappointed that the charge had not been bumped up to attempted murder, but he hoped the end result would be what he wanted.

The crown prosecutor went on to say that given the severity of the charge denying bail was the only option. The accused had not been mandated by the court to be evaluated in a mental facility. He was in the private facility solely at the request of his father after a previous attack on a neighbour.

Millay added that the psychologist charged with evaluating Perkins was on hand and that the crown wanted to call her to testify. The judge agreed. At a nod from the barrister Brenda Castle stood and made her way to the witness stand.

"Dr. Castle," Millay began. "How long have you known Mr. Perkins?"

"Less than two weeks."

"Who asked you to evaluate his mental state?"

"I was contacted by his father's lawyer."

"What exactly was the request?"

"He told me that Garrett had attacked a neighbour who, at the request of Garrett's father, agreed to not press charges as long as Garrett spent some time in an environment where he could deal with his aggressive behaviour."

"How was he progressing?"

"I was still trying to fully assess his progress when he attacked a woman at the hospital."

"He attacked the woman with a knife, correct?"

"Yes."

"Why was he allowed to have a knife in a mental health facility?"

Castle replied that Garrett had obviously sneaked it in without anyone noticing.

"Although you were still getting to know the accused, what was your impression?"

"It was clear that he has impulse control issues. When he wants something, he has to get it right at that moment or he gets angry. I thought he had a lot of work to do before a discharge could be considered."

"However, you were asked to hurry a favourable assessment, were you not?"

"Yes."

"Who asked you?"

"I—rather my husband—was asked to influence me in that direction."

"Who contacted your husband?"

"He told me that is was Garrett's uncle at the request of his sister, Garrett's mother."

The man Sutton had assumed was Garrett's father looked at the woman beside him with a look of disdain that spoke volumes as far as Sutton was concerned. Clearly the parents had different views on how to best deal with their son.

"Did you agree to the request?"

"I didn't have a chance to respond because my husband passed away."

"Thank you, Dr. Castle."

Without waiting for Castle to be excused, Millay addressed the court. "Your Honour, it is quite clear that the accused cannot be released, even in the custody of his parents. He is too dangerous a person to set free at this time. There is no doubt that he will surely continue to be unable to control his emotions."

Millay sat, and the defence solicitor stood to address the court as Brenda Castle returned to her seat.

"Your Honour, Mr. Perkins deeply regrets the incident. The woman was not seriously injured, and while the incident is being investigated his parents will supervise him at home."

"And he will be under tight supervision twenty-four hours a day and getting the regular psychological help he needs?" the judge asked.

"Mr. and Mrs. Perkins are weighing their options at the moment."

"Not good enough, Ms. Curtis," the judge said. "The request for bail is denied. The accused will remain in detention until his trial."

She banged her gavel. "This hearing is closed," she said and quickly left the courtroom.

After letting out a big sigh Sutton could not contain his need to smile. He saw that was also the case for Garrett's father while his mother was frowning and seemingly ready to cry.

Lacrosse had been less than pleased to waste time away from his business interests to come to the hearing but, as was always the case, he couldn't say no to his sister who had saved his life. Years ago, but an event he knew would never be forgotten by either of them. She never missed an opportunity to remind him of the day they had both visited their parents at the request of their mother only to be faced with finding their father drunk, as often happened. He was seated behind the wheel of his car in the driveway while drinking directly from a bottle of whiskey. Joey quickly decided to make his dad aware of his presence by going to stand directly in front of the car. Huge mistake, Ella would later tell her friends.

Their father, seemingly oblivious to his son's presence, started the engine and immediately pressed on the gas pedal. As quickly as if she had been a falcon, Ella pushed her brother out of the way a millisecond before the older Lacrosse sped up and smashed the car against a large maple at the entrance to the driveway.

No doubt because he was drunk, the older Lacrosse was not injured, however it took Joey some time to realize that his own father could easily have killed him had it not been for his sister.

Today, although he was annoyed at having to come to court, he was pleased that his jerk of a nephew had been denied bail. Clearly, the kid needed help to get his head on straight. Lacrosse had liked what the psychologist said and knew that Garrett's dad was the one with the correct view of his son's problems, not his mother. He approached Brenda Castle as she was getting up to leave.

"Dr. Castle, I want to say that I'm sorry for having tried to influence Murray."

"Mr. Lacrosse, let's call a spade a spade. You didn't try to influence my husband, you bullied him. Did you ever think what effect that could have had on him?"

"Are you saying that I contributed to his heart attack? I don't believe that. He had to have other health problems."

Brenda then realized that Lacrosse didn't know about the poison because it had never been published in newspapers or online. And if he was now dealing with another law firm, which she believed, he didn't have occasion to hear the gossip inside her husband's firm. "I don't know. Please excuse me."

As Castle turned on her heels, Sutton opened the door to the court-room for her.

"Detective, you must be pleased with the decision?" she said as she passed through.

They walked together. "Of course. Nice to know that young man won't be able to go near my wife again."

"You are aware I'm sure that Garrett was not specifically targeting your wife. He just could not control his need to make a splash by attacking someone, anyone to show his parents that he can do anything he wants and force them to pay for it. He thinks his dad's money can buy his freedom but I think he's about to hit a wall. Your wife simply happened to be in the wrong place at the wrong time. He will not hurt her again because she's not an impediment in his actions."

"So you don't think he was influenced by Joey Lacrosse to discredit you?"

"As you said, detective, people do all sorts of stupid things, but I don't think it fits here. Lacrosse is much too set on helping his sister to try anything of the sort."

Sutton told her he hoped she was right. When her phone buzzed the detective excused himself and took the stairs down to the street level.

CHAPTER TWENTY-THREE

Sutton and Walters were certain that the man calling himself Henry Fisher had been somehow been unmasked as a viewer of child porn by Murray Castle. They were fairly certain that the man had killed Castle although they didn't have all details in a row just yet on how it was done. Did the man pay someone in Castle's office to drop a pill in the lawyer's pillbox while he was out of the office? That could very well have been the case. If Sutton believed Karen, and he did, because the man had money to buy expensive shoes he certainly could afford paying someone to do his dirty work. Someone is Castle's office?

The pill had to have been put in the pillbox at the office. There was no other explanation.

And as far as Sutton was concerned, Joey Lacrosse had not killed Murray Castle. He had had a row with Castle in frustration for not being able to quickly satisfy his sister's request so he could get back to his businesses. Dr. Brenda Castle had been clear that Lacrosse was a bully not a killer. Besides, she confirmed that Lacrosse had no idea Castle had been murdered.

However, the big question was who did the murderer contact to have a poison pill prepared? The easiest way was to let the culprit tell them, of course, if they could find him.

They now had a sketch of the man but the detectives could not identify him although both thought that he looked familiar in some way. It was a fact of their work that they both met a lot of people every day, so being able to point to one person in particular was almost impossible. After research, they knew that the face didn't have any traits that resembled the lawyers in Murray's firm.

Could it have been a rival lawyer? No, Sutton said as soon as the idea came into his mind because the murder had been too complicated to put together to satisfy a simple case of jealousy.

No, the way it went down indicated a very personal motive.

Now the problem for the detectives was solving the mystery. They needed to step away from the case for a while and come back to it with fresh eyes.

They both turned their attention to other crimes waiting for extra attention.

After several hours of working on felonies other than the Castle murder, Sutton was glad to finally be on his way home. As he drove, he began thinking about what Dr. Maxwell, his wife's psychiatrist, had said about murderers. There is no credible way of predicting whether someone is capable of committing murder, he had said, adding that there aren't any tell-tale signs that a seemingly normal person is on the path to criminality. As an example he had said that when neighbours of those who have committed several murders are interviewed they seem to have the same type of answers: He was quiet, a good neighbour, kept to himself.

Sutton saw that the good doctor had essentially said that it was impossible to predict who could be capable of killing another human being, no matter their role in life. The circumstances were as varied as there were murderers, Maxwell had said, and Sutton certainly agreed.

The circumstances in the Castle case were easy enough to decipher: the murderer feared that his secret would ruin him if it became known. He had probably told Castle that he would give up his addiction, but because he did not want to liberate himself of the pleasure of his obsession, he decided to get rid of the lawyer. No one would ever know if he was wise enough to use a complicated route.

The detective had uncovered the route, now it was a question of discovering the identity of the traveller. No doubt, the culprit was someone of means who probably had never been in trouble with the law, someone well respected within his circle of family, friends and colleagues. An intelligent person. In short a quiet, pleasant neighbour.

Arriving home Sutton decided to put his musings about the Castle case aside for the rest of the evening, he had to turn his attention to other things.

On the days when he did not visit his Anna, Sutton called her in the evening. For him, it was the perfect way to end a day. She had told him earlier that she wouldn't be released for another two days or so. Another disappointment.

"Josh, Dr. Maxwell feels I can leave. It's the other doctor, the one taking care of my wounds. He seems to be afraid that they'll get infected."

"Why would that be? I mean, how?"

"I don't know but he said that if I was discharged, I would have to come back to the hospital anyway to be examined, so it'd be easier for me to stay here for now."

"Looks to me like the hospital is hell bent on taking care of you—like they're afraid of legal action."

"What have you decided about that?"

"I'm not sure how to proceed at this point. I need to get legal advice. It's not something I can decide without knowing all that's involved in suing someone. I've never done it."

"I know you'll make the right decision."

After telling his wife to sleep well, Sutton turned his attention to the hospital. He knew little about it, really, because the insurance had made all the initial arrangements and at that time he wasn't in a frame of mind to ask too many questions. His goal had been for Anna to get the help she needed.

He went to the hospital website which indicated that the private health care facility known as Montrose was owned by the firm Practical Care, Inc., something he already knew although he was not aware of any details about the company. He went to that website and saw that in addition to Montrose, the company owned a dozen care residences for seniors in and around Toronto.

Sutton was aware that many private residences in the province had been investigated because of the number of deaths in their midst during the pandemic however the website made no reference to any such action. The beautiful pictures visually described the residences as modern, clean, airy and full of smiling residents and staff. Obviously it was a privilege to live there. But, Sutton found out upon digging a bit further that only the very wealthy could afford to settle in any of them.

He had never known what Anna's care cost, but he suspected that it was not cheap. They had both been very fortunate that the government had seen fit to help those who dedicated their lives to law and order. But given the limited capabilities of his computer Sutton decided he'd wait until morning to dig further into Practical Care, Inc.

CHAPTER TWENTY-FOUR

Walters had been in touch with the investigators in England about the porn viewer calling himself Henry Fisher informing them that he and his partner still had not yet been able to identify who he really was but were closing in. As a reply, Walters was informed that the British investigation had identified another Canadian child porn site viewer living in Toronto. This man hid his identity more deeply than the man calling himself Henry Fisher. So far, they only knew that he used a no-log virtual private network and that it had been impossible to track who he was. It was frustrating, the man in London said, that they were limited in the efforts of their digital forensic specialists. They could only tell that he was in the greater Toronto area.

Walters promised to investigate and try to find whatever they could. Perhaps by being closer they might have better luck than the British.

After a day of exploration, the two detectives could only claim having hit walls in all direction. Nothing was coming to the surface despite their work on the Castle case. Sutton then turned his attention to Practical Care, Inc.

By digging, he saw the names of the owners of the company. There were three names, and one of them stood out, that of Norbert Perkins.

Had to be Garrett's father, Sutton thought. Sure enough, after more digging, Sutton recognized the man he had seen in court. His bio indicating that he had one son named Garrett and was married to one Ella Lacrosse.

So that's how Garrett ended at Montrose. His dad had simply made a call.

In his research, Sutton came upon an online article relating the history of Montrose. The hospital had been established some thirty years earlier by Joseph Perkins, 'a man of means' the article said, who deplored the lack of help for sufferers of mental problems. The article speculated that the facility, housed in the former home of relatives of Perkins, was essentially geared to the wealthy of Toronto. It hinted at the fact that relatives of the founder had been among the first patients, although the article did not elaborate on that last statement.

So, the detective concluded, Norbert came from money. While Joseph Perkins was still chairman of the board at the hospital, his son was the president. He and a partner had expanded the company into senior care. With a dozen care homes in and around Toronto charging high prices the resulting income for Perkins had to be significant.

Had the company ever been sued? Yes, Sutton found out. Ten families were suing the company for the preventable deaths of older relatives at some of the Perkins private residences during the pandemic. Because all court proceedings had been suspended for a time in order to avoid spreading the virus, the suit had still not been heard by the court. And Sutton could not find any possible timeframe on the upcoming court calendar.

The detective considered that if he sued Montrose, Perkins and his partner would not want to be facing another court appearance. They would surely want to settle or rather Norbert Perkins would probably want to settle as quickly as possible since his own son was the culprit. Sutton was very cognisant that Perkins would not want his partner involved in such a case, a fact that would play in Sutton's favour. But was suing the hospital the right thing to do, he wondered. Anna had been receiving expert care at Montrose. Litigation would tarnish its reputation as one of the best mental care facility in the city.

And he considered that he had to be careful not to hurt the staff at the hospital. If such a case went to trial some of the personnel could be called to testify. That would surely make life miserable for everyone who worked there. Nurse Greta came to mind. A lovely, dedicated soul whose life he didn't want to upset. He had to think about all the ramifications of a legal action especially since he knew that any monetary verdict in his favour would not be especially high. This was Canada after all, not the U.S. where multimillion-dollar settlements seemed to be the norm rather than the exception.

Was it really worth the effort?

Early in the day, while Sutton was just settling in at the division with a large coffee, the black phone on his desk rang. The officer at the reception area told him that a man by the name of Perkins wanted to see him.

As he approached the front of the building Sutton saw Norbert Perkins standing in a corner. The man was impressive. He was tall and burly with abundant black hair without a hint of grey. His face showed an air of superiority, the detective thought.

"Mr. Perkins?"

"Detective, I'd like to talk to you if convenient."

"Of course. Come on back."

Sutton took him to one of the interrogation rooms where they both sat at the table in the middle of the room. "What can we do for you?"

"I know that my son attacked your wife. First, let me say how sorry I am."

Sutton did not know how to comment, so he remained quiet.

"I know your wife has every right to sue him and the hospital and that you may already have begun the process. However, before you go any further I came to tell you that I am ready to offer you a sizeable amount in exchange for your wife signing a waiver foregoing any and all legal action in the matter."

Again, the detective was at a loss for words.

"I know you and your wife need time to think about it and will want to discuss my offer with your lawyer, but I am ready to give you, or rather your wife, a cheque for one-hundred-thousand dollars to save everyone time and money."

"I must say that this is quite a surprise, Mr. Perkins. Of course, I need time ..."

"Of course," Perkins said. "If you accept my offer, your lawyer could get in touch with my lawyer so the assault charges against my son are dropped. And you will have assurances that Garrett will get the help he needs."

"Like the assurances you gave your neighbour—"

Perkins interrupted. "This time I can assure you that he will not be at the Montrose, but in an environment better suited to his needs. I know Garrett has some mental issues but my wife refused to admit that fact until he stabbed your wife. Now she is very much aware of the steps that must be taken. I promise you that our son will not be free until he admits his problems and works at resolving them. And his uncle Joey will not be able to influence the final decision in any way."

"Glad to know," Sutton said.

Perkins stood and dropped a business card on the table in front of Sutton. "Call me anytime, hopefully very soon."

He offered his hand, and Sutton took it as he also stood. Obviously the meeting was over.

As he escorted Perkins out of the division, Sutton could only consider that the moneyed felt they had a right to manipulate others. Of course a sizeable unexpected amount of money would be marvellous, Josh Sutton thought.

He and Anna had earned everything they had accumulated. His dad, a man who loved his work as a mechanic and serviced cars in his own garage, would not be giving Josh a fortune like Joseph Perkins had entrusted to Norbert. But the older Sutton had raised Josh and his sister to be, foremost, honest and caring which eventually lead Josh to choose a career in law enforcement and his sister to become a nurse.

CHAPTER TWENTY-FIVE

In early afternoon, Sutton and Walters made their way to the offices of Mercer Davis Carroll and Castle. As usual the receptionist welcomed them with a bright smile.

"Mr. Mercer is waiting for you," she informed the detectives.

Gabriel Mercer stood to welcome his visitors after his assistant opened the door and showed the two men in.

"Come on in and sit," Mercer invited.

Sutton spoke: "As I said on the phone we want to find out if you, or your partners, or the other lawyers in your firm can identify a man from a sketch."

"We'll try," Mercer said as Walters pulled out a copy of Karen's sketch from a thin plastic folder he had been carrying. He put it in front of the lawyer.

Mercer's facial movements revealed nothing. After a moment or two he said that he could have seen the man, but because of the number of people he met in his role as a barrister he certainly could not identify him.

The detectives didn't expect that the lawyers would be able to identify the suspect immediately however they were betting that if they saw him again, they might remember the sketch.

"Did this man have something to do with Murray's murder?"

"We are not sure at this point, but we do believe he had a run-in with Murray Castle shortly before he died," Walters said.

"Really?"

"We'd like to leave you a copy of the sketch to, perhaps, help you remember," Sutton said. "If, however, you can identify him, please do not inform him that we're looking for him."

"Of course. It goes without saying," Mercer said.

Sutton pointed out that they wanted to show the sketch to the other lawyers in case they knew the man.

"I've already advised everyone of your visit, so go ahead." He picked up his phone to call Cecilia. In a moment the assistant appeared, and Walters went with her to test everyone's recollection.

Sutton remained seated. "I need to consult a lawyer on a personal matter, and I'm wondering when would be a good time for me to put some questions to you."

"If it won't take too long, we could do it right now."

"Great," Sutton exclaimed. "As you surely know, Joey Lacrosse's nephew stabbed my wife—"

"What? You can't be serious? When did this happen?"

"A couple days ago. She's mending and will be okay."

"Thank goodness!"

"The young man, the nephew, is the son of Lacrosse's sister who married into a wealthy family. Her husband has offered me a hundred grand in exchange for my wife not pressing charges. The young man has been denied bail."

"Wow!" Mercer exclaimed.

"Is this legal? Is it ethical? If I may add, for us extra money would be very welcome."

"Believe me, I fully understand," Mercer said. After a brief pause he continued. "In civil litigation lawyers make monetary deals all the time. They settle, as it were, so they don't have to go to court and risk losing. Here, it'll be filed as a criminal offense not a civil one. I suggest you contact the crown prosecutor in the case and get his or her input. They will be able to guide you quickly."

"Thank you, Mr. Mercer. I appreciate your advice. How much do I owe you?"

Mercer smiled. "Detective, you're working at finding the murderer who killed my friend Murray Castle. I'm the one who owes you, believe me."

Sutton appreciated the remark, thanked Mercer and went to the reception area to wait for his colleague who appeared just a few minutes later.

No, Walters reported, no one in the office seemed to know the identity of the man.

When Sutton closed up shop for the day he made his way to the hospital. He had a lot to discuss with Anna. Hopefully, Greta would be able to feed him.

CHAPTER TWENTY-SIX

Ella Perkins had another of her headaches. She had been suffering with headaches every day since Garrett had been denied bail and, as a result, went to bed early, something that pleased Norbert. He was getting tired of fighting with his wife and loved being left to entertain himself in the evening. The problem with Ella was that she could not accept that her child had mental problems. It shamed her. Norbert understood and sympathized with her, but at the same time he was cognisant that mental illness was part of his family's legacy that led to the establishment of Montrose.

Of course, that didn't mean that he was pleased with the current Garrett situation. If his pitch to the detective earlier in the day bore results, his son would get the care he needed without a trial the media was sure to milk for all it could.

Norbert didn't mind being on his own in the evening, in fact it suited him well especially at this time. His computer was a blessed release from all the problems at home and those that sprang up day after day at the office.

Decades earlier, when home computers began appearing on the market, Norbert had bought the most advanced type at the time. He taught himself everything he could about this marvellous new machine that was becoming part of the landscape in offices and in homes everywhere. It fascinated him. It was even more captivating after the internet became a necessity.

He wanted to spend his life working with computers but Joseph, his father, had other plans. He needed Norbert to contribute to the management of Montrose while he devoted himself to the building of another wing to satisfy the demand for mental health care among the elite. The father won the discussion and Norbert went to business school which would eventually lead him to see that the care of seniors was a sector needing more and more players as the population continued to age. And it had proven to be a lucrative enterprise.

He had been right on, but over the years he still managed to satisfy his love of everything related to computerization. It became an all consuming hobby as new operating systems and possibilities appeared on the market and in his home. He learned it all by himself.

Ella did not like to see a large monitor, a printer and peripheral cables in her den. She could travel the net and send emails from her small laptop surely Norbert should be able to do the same. But after much discussion Norbert agreed to relocate his hobby to a room in the basement. After he had moved the stacked boxes out of the way into another smaller room, he soon realized that this new location was ideal.

After the move, being far from Ella when indulging in his hobby made him feel freer. Whenever he worked in the den, she seemed to be always poking her head in to ask questions or discuss whatever was on her mind. In the basement he was only interrupted for emergencies.

It had been a rough few days for Norbert and he needed release. He did what he always did when the pressure was in danger of exploding: he relied on his digital expertise. In a minute he was on his no-log virtual private network where the many levels of encryption made it impossible for law enforcement to track him. He knew he could visit any site without fear of being identified by even the best digital forensic examiner. Because he knew that in Canada viewing of child porn was a criminal offense with a possible sentence of as much as two years he took all possible precautions so that his hobby would remain private.

In a moment, he saw that one website had been blocked. He figured the police had discovered it, but that didn't stop Norbert. There were plenty of other sites he could visit where no one could find him. When he was admitted on one site, he looked at a video that was especially pornographic. Norbert loved looking at those, but he did not abuse children nor take photos of them, and he never wasted time chatting with others on those types of sites. Deep down he knew he was a voyeur and that it was a mental illness no doubt inherited through family genes, but his hobby did not hurt anyone and helped him cope with life's problems.

He had long ago convinced himself that it was better than being a drunk.

Better for his liver, in any case.

CHAPTER TWENTY-SEVEN

Sutton had been fortunate that Greta had an extra plate of quiche and salad for him just like the one Anna was enjoying at the table under the window when he joined her in her room. Greta smiled at him, saying that she knew it would his night to visit. He told her how great she was, and he was sure she blushed a little.

"Gonna miss Anna," she said as she left the room.

They both enjoyed the meal, and Anna was pleased to confirm that doctors had finally decided that she would be released the very next day. Her wounds were healing very well, and she couldn't wait to go home. She had already contacted her mother who would be there for her during the day as long as needed. Anna's parents lived just twenty minutes away, so travel time was not an issue.

With the good news out of the way, Josh brought up something that could also be good news: the offer from Norbert Perkins. Anna could not believe what her husband was telling her.

"You mean to tell me that the guy's father wants to give us a hundred-thousand dollars so we don't press charges?"

Josh pointed out that that was the deal, essentially. There was, of course, the requirement of a signed affidavit to the effect that she would not sue.

"Is there anything in the law that would prevent our accepting such an offer?" she asked.

"I was thinking of talking it over with captain Corbett, see what he thinks." After a pause, he added: "It'd be nice to have extra money, don't you think? I mean it'd help if we're going to have a couple of kids. Maybe move to a larger house."

Smiling, she agreed that it would and opened her arms for his embrace.

Early the next morning, Josh Sutton was sitting across the desk from captain Corbett.

"That's great news," Corbett commented when Sutton told him Anna was being released. "Take the rest of the day to take care of your wife."

"Thank you. Captain, I need to ask you something."

"Sure. Shoot."

"Is it ethical for a policeman's wife to accept money in exchange for not pressing charges for an incident which is in no way related to his work?"

Sutton was surprised when his superior said: "I guess Perkins got to you, didn't he?"

"You know?" Sutton exclaimed.

"Simple deduction. I saw Perkins in here yesterday. I know his son has been in trouble before, and I suspect he wants to avoid the publicity of a trial."

"What do you suggest I do? Extra money would be nice."

"Everybody can use more money. Talk to the crown prosecutors and work it out with them."

Sutton thanked the captain and left.

As he was driving toward the hospital he was well aware that he had been expecting his captain to throw a wrench in his hope of getting extra money rather than the reaction he got. Of course, nothing was settled yet, but it could be soon.

Anna Sutton left Montrose all smiles, on the arm of her detective husband. She had cried earlier as she had said goodbye to the staff who had taken care of her as well as a few patients and the women in her informal yoga class. She planned to stay in touch with two of them. One of them had killed her young child by accident and was being supervised so she didn't kill herself. The second one was being waned from using anti-anxiety prescribed medication she'd been taken since her husband's death years earlier. Anna had liked both of the women and told them she expected them to be able to join her for a meal outside the hospital within a few weeks. They both agreed they would do their best.

Anna was pleased that she would continue to see Dr. Maxwell on a non-formal schedule after she'd settled in and seen her son's room, or whenever she felt the need.

Her warmest comments were reserved for Greta who had made Anna's afternoons and early evenings more pleasant than would otherwise have been the case.

Stepping outside in the spring air, Anna felt elated which made Josh feel better than he had in months. They were turning over a new leaf and it was indeed delightful for both of them.

Anna almost screamed with joy when she saw their house. How lovely it was, and it was waiting for her. Josh got her bag as she stepped out of the car and looked around. The peonies would be blooming again soon, and she couldn't wait to plant some annuals to brighten the front of their home.

She stepped inside almost cautiously which worried Josh for a moment. "It's exciting," Anna said. "Coming home."

"You don't know how happy it makes me," Josh added.

Once inside she walked around the house taking it all in as if she was seeing everything for the first time. When she came to the door to their son's room she hesitated a moment but did not go in. Perhaps tomorrow, she told herself.

They ate lunch in the sunroom at the back enjoying the quietness of the cedar hedge and the two tall maples surrounding the property. Josh had ordered submarines the previous evening and served them with the hot tea Anna enjoyed. The conversation was light but a bit strained because both ignored the very real spirit of their son.

After Anna had unpacked and settled in, Josh wanted to know if she was ready for a walk in the warm sunshine. Not quite yet, she replied. First she wanted to open the door to Bryan's room because Dr. Maxwell had told her that she had to do it as soon as possible. The more she hesitated the more difficult it was bound to become.

They walked down the hall together, hand in hand, and she very slowly opened the door to the child's room. Anna put a hand over her mouth to stifle a scream. It was exactly like it was when their little boy left for the hospital, never to come back. Suddenly her eyes filled with tears and Josh put an arm around her shoulders. Unexpectedly, she freed herself from her husband and fled away.

He found her in a corner of the living room, her shaking body rolled into a ball just as she often did before going to Montrose. All he could think of was that the nightmare was back full force.

CHAPTER TWENTY-EIGHT

Josh Sutton took one of his wife's hands and slowly tried to get her back on her feet. She resisted at first, but then let herself be led to the beige sofa. He sat close to her and put his arms around her in an attempt to stop the shaking, wondering if she had left the hospital too soon.

"I'm here. We'll get through this together," he said in a soft voice.

The warmth of his body helped her stop the shaking, and she let her head fall on his shoulder. "I'm sorry."

"It's okay. Let's just rest a minute."

She sighed, willing herself to be stronger, then said: "Dr. Maxwell told me it would be difficult at first but that I couldn't give up. I feel that I should try again."

"I'll be right beside you."

They stood together and again slowly walked down the hall. This time Josh opened the door and pushed it all the way in as they both stood outside looking in. It took a few minutes but Anna walked slowly into the room, taking time to look at everything, from the bed to the toys on the floor.

"I miss him so much!" she said in a teary voice as she continued to inspect the remnants of Bryan's life.

"Honey, of course you do. Just like I miss him, but we have to concentrate on the memories now. He was a great kid and we were fortunate to be able to cherish him for six years."

"Why weren't we allowed to cherish him forever?"

"I wish I knew! But I think that instead of focusing on our pain we should consider that he is now an angel," Josh said. "He can't be anything but an angel."

"That's such a nice way of putting it."

"He's an angel who watches over us. That's the way I've been willing myself to think of him."

Anna approached Josh and he took her into his arms. "Josh you're so much stronger than I am, so much more clear headed. I'll try to be more positive. I know I've caused you a lot of trouble, and for that I apologize."

He kissed the top of her head. "Don't worry. You were never trouble. It's all good."

A few minutes after his mother-in-law arrived to support Anna, Josh went back to work. He figured it'd be better if the two women cried and took care of each other without him, especially because he found it more and more difficult to see Anna cry over their son. He could only hope that she would make an effort to be positive as she had promised.

That was essential if they were to have another child.

He was on his way to the division when he pulled his car into a filling station, parking away from the pumps. There he called Neil Millay, the assistant crown prosecutor in the Perkins file, and asked for an appointment. Millay said he could see him in an hour or so. That gave Josh time to get all the way downtown Toronto to the McMurtry-Scott building and walk around a little to prepare himself for the meeting.

Once seated across the desk from Millay, Josh Sutton simply said that since his wife was involved, he was curious as to developments in the Perkins case.

"We're still trying to see how to proceed."

"Could my wife ask that the charges be withdrawn?"

"I don't understand why she thinks she could do it. In any event what would she say? That Garrett didn't really knife her? Then who did? There are witnesses and the provincial health records indicate that she was treated for knife wounds." Millay stared at Sutton for a moment. "Am I right that Garrett's father is putting pressure on you because he wants to avoid a trial?"

Sutton hesitated while he deliberated whether he should confide in the assistant crown prosecutor. Truth won out. "Yes, he did. He offered us money in exchange for my wife withdrawing the charges."

"I see. First of all, our office is the only one that can withdraw charges after bail has been denied if and when we see that there is not enough evidence to get a conviction. Right now it's clear that the young man needs psychiatric help. We'll be talking to his attorney, Lisa Curtis, because we believe she wants to have Perkins properly assessed by a psychiatrist in a closed environment for a period of time. The result will guide us as to how to proceed. Depending on the conclusions we might very well ask the court for Garrett to be committed for a period of time without going to trial."

"When will you be talking to Ms. Curtis?"

"We have a meet scheduled for tomorrow morning. The gossip is that she is also being pressured by the young man's father to avoid a trial, so I think that Garrett Perkins will most certainly be released from custody into a mental institution. I can call you once the meeting is over so you know what's going on."

"That'd be great. Thanks."

"Josh, can I talk frankly?"

"Of course."

"I suspect that you're having a serious debate with your conscience over the money offer. I can see why. You're an honest man, but extra money would go a long way in making up for your wife's suffering, right?" Josh nodded. "Let me make it easy for you. No matter what happens, whether this case goes to trial or not, your wife can sue the young man in civil court to get monetary compensation for her suffering, etcetera. As you know, the amount awarded might not be great—this is Canada after all—but the family would have to hire a lawyer and then it becomes a question of your wife negotiating with the lawyer. If the family is set on avoiding publicity, a deal could be reached quickly. This type of negotiation happens all the time in civil cases."

Josh Sutton could not avoid a smile of relief. "Good to know," he said simply.

Neil Millay wished the detective good luck as he shook his hand.

Sutton was tempted to do a little victory dance as he left the building.

CHAPTER TWENTY-NINE

When Josh Sutton answered his phone the next morning, he hadn't expected to hear from his caller so early.

"Josh, here's what happening," Millay said. "Perkins' lawyer, Lisa Curtis, wants her client to be assessed as soon as possible so that his mental acuity is established. As I told you, we believe Garrett's father is pressuring her to avoid a trial at all cost. In any event, we've decided to go along. We're scheduled to appear before a judge sometime tomorrow."

"Really," was all Sutton could say.

"I'm telling you this because I'm sure you might want to be there."

"Definitely."

Norbert Perkins was the only other person in the gallery when Sutton entered the courtroom the next day. The detective arrived a couple minutes before the judge, the Honourable Harold Evers, entered and took his seat. Josh instantly remembered the photo he saw on the grand piano when he had interviewed the judge's wife, Constance Carroll. The jurist had a round face crowned by short mostly grey curly hair and wore the traditional black robe, white tabs and red sash of Ontario judges. He looked at the defendant's lawyer then at the assistant crown prosecutor before calling on the defence to address the court.

Sutton hardly heard how Lisa Curtis presented her arguments. He was consumed with examining judge Evers. There was something about the man that Sutton couldn't quite reach to put into words. However, when the judge had to read a document and put on a pair of black-framed glasses, Karen's sketch jumped in front of his mind's eyes. Could the judge be Henry Fisher? No, he admonished himself. She had drawn a man with straight mostly black hair. This fellow definitely had curly grey hair and Karen had been sure that Henry Fisher did not wear a wig.

Let it go for now and concentrate on the proceeding in front of you, he reminded himself.

Now he was listening to Millay who was telling the judge that the crown agreed with the defence that since Garrett Perkins had been in a mental health facility at the time of the attack that a further assessment of the young man would ensure a proper resolution of the case.

In what seemed a minute later, the judge granted the motion for a psychiatric evaluation of the mental state of the accused, then quickly left the courtroom.

Neil Millay turned briefly and nodded to Sutton who acknowledged the gesture with a nod of his own. As the detective stood up he saw that Norbert Perkins was in deep discussion with his son's attorney. He made his way out. If Perkins wanted to talk, he knew where the detective worked.

During his lunch break, Ross Walters made a point of calling his sister Tiana who had texted that she was inviting him to dinner the following Saturday.

"Of course, I'll be there. Wouldn't miss it. Haven't seen you in a while. In any case what's the occasion?"

"It's Delon's birthday. Your only nephew."

"Of course he's my only nephew. You're my only sister and you kept insisting on giving birth to girls."

"Just like it was my decision!"

"Kidding, Tia. What kind of gift would he like?"

"He's got enough computer stuff, so nothing electronic. A gift card of some sort would be something he'd like."

"What about a ticket to a Maple Leafs game?"

"Those are too expensive for a birthday gift," Tiana commented.

"Not a problem because I just won a pair in a draw at the gym where I work out."

"Wow. That'd be a hit for sure, but wouldn't you prefer to go with one of your buddies, or one of your many lady friends?"

"No. I think they should be shared with family. See you Saturday."

Sutton had barely made it back to his division when the officer at the reception advised him that a man by the name of Perkins asked to see him. The detective took Norbert to one of the interrogation rooms.

"So you saw this morning that Garrett will be getting the help he needs. That's what I wanted, as you know, but it came from an angle that was not exactly what I had anticipated."

The previous evening, Josh and Anna had come to the conclusion that after the court decision it would certainly mean no trial. So surely Perkins would withdraw his offer to them, but Josh believed they could still sue in civil court. Anna wasn't sure she'd be willing to testify. She'd think about it, she had told her husband.

As he was waiting for confirmation that Perkins' offer was rescinded, the big man surprised Josh.

"That does not mean that I don't owe your wife, and you, compensation. I'm fully aware that you can sue Garrett and the hospital in civil court. In order to avoid the trouble of both sides having to hire lawyers and waste time in court, I've decided to honour my original offer of a hundred thousand dollars. The only request is for your wife to sign an affidavit to the effect that the amount is satisfactory compensation for her injuries and that she will not pursue a court action now or later."

Sutton's work had trained him to avoid showing emotion with facial expressions, something he was doing now sitting across from Perkins. "Let me discuss it with my wife. After all she was the victim of your son's actions."

"Of course. Call me as soon as you can." And with those words, Perkins stood. Again, like the previous time, he was ending the meeting. Sutton accompanied him back to the main entrance.

As he was driving away, Norbert Perkins was relieved that that one particular problem had been solved. At least, his son would be getting help despite what his wife Ella wanted, and Joey Lacrosse would no longer be playing games to satisfy his sister.

Norbert had often wanted to say to his brother-in-law: Joey, you've paid your sister back many times for her having saved your life. Let it go now once and for all, otherwise Ella will continue to guilt you whenever she wants something!

He hoped to have the courage to do it now that Garrett was where he needed to be. That would clear his mind for the other problems he faced.

Now that the pandemic was history, legal cases launched against senior care homes in Ontario by family members of victims were already in line to proceed. Most people thought it was more than time since the majority of deaths due to the pandemic had occurred in long-term care homes.

The ten suits against Perkins' company would come up sooner rather than later now that the judicial machine was now fully back on track. He knew his company would be studied with a fine tooth comb by the media, and that personnel would be interviewed along with current residents. It would come out that one of the reasons the deadly virus circulated freely in his residences was the high turnover among caretakers and orderlies always looking for better pay and benefits. And there was also the inadequate number of employees. That, the media had concluded, was the case in a lot of private care homes where the treatment of elderly people had been qualified as "deeply disturbing."

That lack of personnel Norbert blamed solely on his partner who was always searching for ways to increase their profit even when the staff found the work stressful. It had been a risky move that could now result in being a serious blow to their bottom line if they were found responsible for the deaths, and their insurer was as stingy as most are, he thought.

And adding to his worries was the fact that some of the families suing his company were comprised of law enforcement personnel as well as lawyers. The road ahead would be anything but smooth.

He would go home early today and find solace in looking at the forbidden pictures.

CHAPTER THIRTY

Ross Walters always enjoyed spending time with his sister Tiana and her brew: a husband, a son, and three girls. They shared an excellent meal of grilled salmon and vegetables, followed by a cake adorned with twenty candles. After Delon had extinguished them came the gifts. When he opened the card from his uncle and saw the two hockey tickets to a Maple Leafs game against their long-time rival Montreal Canadiens for the following weekend, Delon was ecstatic.

"Thanks, uncle Ross. You gonna come with me or do I invite my girl?"

Tiana's ears perked up. "You got a girl? You didn't tell me. Why is that?"

"Because she's just a friend. Anyway, she's not into hockey."

"I guess you're stuck with me, Delon. Are you still into computers?" Walters asked.

Everyone groaned.

"Ross, you know better than to ask a question like that. He'll go on for the rest of the night with his exploits on the computer," Delon's father commented.

Delon paid no attention to his father and talked to his uncle. "I can show you my new stuff downstairs."

"That'd be great."

And with those words the two fellows made their way to the corner of the basement where there was an array of electronic gadgets including two monitors.

"Why do you need two monitors?" Ross asked.

"Because when I'm working on something, I may need to research something else." "Your mom tells me you're about ready to teach computer programming."

"Yeah. My training is done, just need to ace some tests so I can teach the basics. For now. I'll be starting in the fall. Can't wait."

"It amazes me what you have accomplished with computers at your young age."

"Uncle Ross, I'm old compared to the geniuses coming up."

Ross Walters couldn't help sighing. "If you're old, what am I?"

"You's police. Totally different."

Delon's fingers were busy on a keyboard as multi screen shots began appearing on one of the monitors.

"What are all those?"

"Shots of kids coming and going outside a school. I shot those at the request of the school using a drone. Because they don't have cameras all around the building, they wanted to know what kids did during breaks. As you can see, some smoke weed, others ... get hot and heavy..." he coughed.

"You mean have sex," Ross offered.

"Right."

An idea suddenly came into Ross Walters' mind. "Tell me something, Delon. You can do almost anything on a computer, can't you?"

"Sure. Why you ask?"

"Could you, for example, break into a no-log virtual private network?"

"What you doing on the dark web, uncle Ross?"

"We're trying to identify a paedophile who uses it."

Delon hesitated a moment. "I've learned how to bypass some impressive firewalls," he chuckled. "I suppose I better not tell the police!"

"The police heard nothing."

After another moment Delon added: "I've learned to navigate everything on the web, white, deep or black. The prob with private networks is it's almost impossible to follow the misdirection they travel. Besides, criminals use them, so I leave them alone."

"But it could be done?"

"Maybe. You asking if I could find him?"

"It would help us stop the man. However, what I'm telling you must never be repeated."

"No worries, uncle Ross," the young man said as he passed his fingers over his mouth. "But why d'you think I'm better than a bunch of police computer geniuses?" Not waiting for an answer, he added: "Because the police... they have to follow rules, even with the dark web browser. Right?"

"Delon, you're too smart for your own good. Can it be done without attracting attention?"

"If you know how. Besides, I owe you. You talked to my parents when they were set on my becoming something important like a lawyer or a doctor," he said gesturing with air quotes. "If I can find a paedophile, that'd be important, no?"

"For sure, but you can't ever tell them. Promise?"

"Promise."

"You won't be spending time on porn sites, will you?"

"I'm old enough to know what's going on in the world, uncle Ross. Don't worry. I have no interest in porn of any kind."

"Glad to know. I'll be in touch with the info you'll need to get started."

Josh Sutton was frustrated that they were not progressing rapidly in the Castle case. He could not see a clear road in addition to being still bothered by the fact that judge Evers reminded him of Karen's sketch. It seemed impossible that a judge could be a pervert. But then again perverts came in all sizes and ages as he had found out over the years.

Relying on the site showing pictures of all the Ontario magistrates, he brought up a photo of the judge and enlarged it. He then brought up Karen's sketch and studied both. He could almost swear that the honourable judge was Henry Fisher, a miserable paedophile. One of the main difference in the two visuals was the hair. Could Karen have been mistaken?

Possibly.

One question in Sutton's mind was if the judge was Henry Fisher why would he use a library computer instead of private networks. Whenever he went to the library and got on the dark web through the router, he was risking being exposed if someone saw what he was watching online.

Then, remembering from the online bio of the judge that he and his wife funded camps for children, beads of sweat began appearing on Josh's forehead. That couldn't be, could it? Could a superior court judge be abusing children right under everyone's nose?

And if that were the case, it meant that his wife, the highly regarded barrister Constance Carroll, would have had the opportunity to poison her law partner.

Wow, Josh thought. Were he right, the Toronto judicial elite was in for a shock.

Josh sent Karen's digital sketch to Pete, their artist, then went to see him.

"Hello again, detective. What can I do for you today?"

"Are you busy?"

"Never too busy to help you. What do you need?"

"I just sent you a sketch, and would like you to alter it so the man has short curly grey hair instead of what's there now."

"No problem. I'll have it for you first thing tomorrow."

CHAPTER THIRTY-ONE

When Josh Sutton came home, he was happy to see that Anna seemed calm as she greeted him with a kiss. He saw that she had an apron tied around her waist over jeans and a white tee while the aroma of chicken cacciatore was very pleasing to his olfactory organ. It was definitely one of his favourite dishes, especially the way she prepared it.

"You've been busy, I smell," he commented.

She chuckled. "It's so nice to be back in my kitchen. Had to make something special for you to make up for all the trouble I caused."

As a response he held her close and kissed the top of her head.

"Why don't you get changed while I finish what I was doing."

"Yes, ma'am. Where's your mother?"

"She went home. I think she was a bit tired after going shopping with me for food and supplies."

When he returned after a shower wearing chinos and a tee, Anna had the dining room table all set up for a meal with a large platter of chicken in its mushroom and tomato sauce sitting between the two place settings. There was even a bouquet of spring flowers in the middle of the table. Life was promising to be on an upswing, Josh thought.

They shared the delicious meal as they discussed ways of embellishing the yard near the house with flowers and bushes. After the meal

Josh helped his wife clean up, and when they were enjoying their coffee, he broached the subject of money.

"Norbert Perkins came to see me today. His son's lawyer got the court to agree that he needed to be in a closed environment where he could get help, rather than in a prison setting. I thought Norbert would withdraw his money offer, but he didn't. He will give us a cheque for one-hundred-thousand dollars in exchange for you signing a paper to the effect that it is a satisfactory compensation for his son's attack and that you will not take legal action against him or the hospital, now or later."

"Is that ethical and legal?"

"The crown prosecutor assures me it is in civil cases. What do you say? Will you sign?"

"You don't really expect me to say no, do you?"

"Then we can make plan for a vacation somewhere. I could get away as soon as we close the case we're working on."

"Where do you want me to sign?"

The next morning, as Josh Sutton opened his email he saw that Pete had gotten back to him. When he clicked on the attachment and the reworked sketch appeared on the screen, the detective had no doubt that judge Evers was Henry Fisher.

He called Ross Walters over.

"What's up?"

"Look at what's on my screen," Sutton said.

Walters took several moments to assess the new sketch. "That's judge Evers!"

"Damn right."

"Eureka! What do we do now?"

"Bring him in for questioning," Sutton said.

"I'd like to inform my London contact first. They were the ones investigating and could tell us if he uploaded videos of children so our case is tight."

"I doubt he could upload anything while working in a library."

"He might have been able to do it if he had the video on a USB key," Walters put in.

"Okay, talk to your contact. If he uploaded videos of children we need to investigate if the good judge has been filming the children who spend time at the summer camps he and his wife sponsor."

"Hard to prove if it's true, but it would make sense that he would. Before going further we have to make sure we have all the proof in a neat row. He's a judge after all."

"I hear you," Sutton said. "And I pity the poor prosecutor who's assigned to the case!"

"In the meantime we're almost ready to arrest them both for poisoning Murray Castle. Evers most probably had the aconite pill made and then his wife put it in Castle's little pill box when he was out of his office. We need more proof, of course."

"You think his wife knew he was a child pornographer?"

"She may be one herself. We have to find out."

"But how did Castle find out about the judge's dirty secret?" Walters asked.

"In the library?" Sutton offered hopefully.

Soon, Sutton saw one of the division's uniformed officers approach with a letter-size envelope in her hands.

"A courier left this for you at the front. I thought I'd save you some steps," the young officer said as she put the envelope on the detective's desk.

Sutton thanked the woman and slid the envelope open. It contained only one sheet of paper displaying the name and address of a local law firm the detective did not know. The text on the letter stated that the sum of one-hundred-thousand dollars Anna Sutton received from Garrett Perkins was adequate compensation for the injuries and pain suffered at his hands. It further stated that Anna agreed to not sue the Montrose hospital with regard to the incident now or in the future.

Josh Sutton was pleased. A nice bonus was in the offing. He put the letter back in the envelope to bring home to his wife.

Turning back to the case at hand, Sutton needed to follow the trail Murray Castle had left behind that could prove the reason for his murder. He called the offices the Mercer Davis Carroll and Castle and asked for Cecilia.

"Oh, hello detective," she said after he identified himself.

"I need your help."

"Of course. Anything."

"I assume you still have the details of Murray Castle's day-to-day appointments?"

"Yes, I do. The partners want all the information relative to Mr. Castle's activities kept in a special data file," she replied.

"You always knew where he was meeting clients, didn't you?"

"Of course. It's a rule here that partners must know where all the lawyers are."

"Good. I would like you to look over his appointments outside the office in the three months prior to his death and see if he ever met anyone at a Toronto library."

"Right away I can tell you that he did. More than once, however I don't remember who or how often but I'll find out for you."

"Thank you, Cecilia. We appreciate your help."

"I liked Mr. Castle and I want to know who killed him, so I'm happy to help you."

CHAPTER THIRTY-TWO

Ross Walters was getting to his car after a full day of investigation when his phone buzzed. He saw that it was his nephew Delon.

"What's doing Delon?"

"Can you come by when you're off work. I got something for you."

"Okay. Half an hour," Walters said figuring that's how long it would take him to make it to his sister's suburban home. That detour meant he would be late for dinner with his date, the gorgeous actress a friend had introduced him to. But he was certain she would understand because her old man was a policeman in Vancouver. She knew all about work taking priority over personal plans. He called her, and she did understand.

When he rang the doorbell, his sister Tiana answered.

"Ross! Nice surprise," she said hugging him briefly. "Dinner's almost ready. Join us."

"Thanks for the invite but I've got a date."

"Of course. What was I thinking!"

"I'm just stopping by to see Delon."

"What are you two cooking up."

"I just asked him for some information, that's all."

"He's downstairs."

Delon was busy in front of one of his monitors and didn't hear his uncle approach until he called his name.

"Hi, uncle Ross. I got something for you. I did a lot of traveling on the web and I've got to say it was all... interesting... or rather informative. Saw lots of stuff I didn't think—"

"Existed," his uncle interrupted. "You know that the web's the biggest garbage dump the world has ever known."

"Yeah, but don't worry I've already forgotten about it. How do you deal with seeing all those kids ..."

"Like you did, we forget about it. Anyway, what did you find?"

"The network was very good at covering the tracks of its subscribers, but the man in Toronto left a clue and I got him. I don't think he understands everything about how the progression of computerization works. Here," Delon said, getting a piece a paper from his work table. I printed the info for you."

"Thanks. Didn't take you long. What!" Walters exclaimed as he read the name. "Are you sure?"

"Very sure, uncle Ross. Why? Someone you know?"

"Oh, yeah. Thanks so much, Delon. Still on for the hockey game?"

"Always."

"To thank you for helping us, we'll grab dinner before the game."

"Cool."

It was just after nine o'clock the next morning when Sutton got a call back from Cecilia, the late Murray Castle's assistant.

"Detective, I found the information you wanted. Mr. Castle met with a client twice in the Etobicoke library. The client was a woman who's part owner of a ladies clothing store and wanted to meet Mr. Castle somewhere where they wouldn't be seen. She was planning to buy out her partner and was afraid of leaks. Is that what you were looking for?"

"Yes. When did the meetings take place?"

"Both in March, the 20th and the 29th. I know Mr. Castle prepared all the necessary papers, but I don't know what happened to the transaction since then."

"Thank you, very much, Cecilia. This helps a great deal. I will keep you informed about our investigation."

He was just hanging up when Walters came into his office.

"Have you finished your transaction with Perkins?"

"Almost. Anna has signed the paper," he said pointing to the envelope on his desk. "Why do you ask?"

"I don't want to tell you my news until you do finalize with Perkins."

"What's with the cloak and dagger stuff? Perkins's coming by in a couple of hours."

"Let's talk when you're done," Walters said and walked out.

What the hell? Sutton thought. Definitely not like Ross to keep him in the dark, but he did respect his judgment. Besides, there was lots to do in the next couple of hours.

Norbert Perkins arrived at the division less than two hours later. He and Sutton met in one of the interrogation rooms. Sutton handed him the duly signed affidavit, Perkins briefly looked it over than reached into his jacket pocket and handed Sutton an envelope containing a bank draft payable to Anna Sutton in the agreed-to amount. Although the detective expected the money, he was still somewhat surprised that it actually came to pass.

"Thank you," was all he could say to Perkins.

"I'm the one who needs to thank you. I'm sure you aware of the legal actions taken against my company following the deaths of some of our residents during the pandemic. If there was to be a legal action against Montrose, it could be disastrous for us. This way my son gets the help he desperately needs and the hospital's reputation will not be sullied."

With that comment, the big man stood and offered his hand to Sutton. The detective shook it and accompanied Perkins to the division's entrance.

"I hope your wife's recovery will continue without problems," Perkins offered as he left.

Back in his office, Sutton folded the envelope Perkins had given him and put it in the inside pocket of his suit jacket before signalling to Walters to join him.

"So, what's going on, Ross?"

"Hold on to your britches. The second guy from Toronto who got on private child porn networks is Norbert Perkins," Walters said.

"How in the hell do you know that?"

"The London people could only go so far, so I asked Delon, my nephew. I told you about him. He's a computer whiz."

"Your nephew!"

"Either that or we would never have known."

"And now if we need to have proof of how we found out he's into child porn, what do we do?"

"No worries. London knows that Perkins only looked. He never uploaded videos or did any chatting with others on the sites he visited like those people usually do. He was not an active perpetrator. Nevertheless accessing child porn is an indictable offense in Canada with a minimum of one year in jail."

"In my dealings with Perkins, I certainly never saw any sign of abject depravity." Sutton commented. "Let's send this to the crown along with the info from London and let the chips fall where they may."

"I'll take care of it," Walters offered.

"And you asked me if I had concluded my business with Perkins because?"

"I didn't want you to be distracted when you saw him, that's all."

"Thanks. But knowing what he does in his spare time is very disconcerting. Maybe I should give the money back."

"Unless I'm mistaken, the money is from Garrett to Anna for her pain and suffering, so it has actually little to do with Norbert or you. If I were you I would forget about Norbert. He's an emotionally deprived man with a mental disorder. I predict that his obsession will get him into trouble one of day very soon."

"Wise words," Sutton commented, and Walters simply smiled.

CHAPTER THIRTY-THREE

Sutton and Walters made their way to the Etobicoke library. Soon, after showing their identifications to one of the ladies manning the circulation counter, they were invited to sit across the desk from the head librarian a no-nonsense woman in her fifties who smiled warmly at the two detectives.

"Detective Sutton, I remember the name. You were here before and left your card which ended up on my desk. What can we do for you today?"

"We need information that should be easy for you to provide. We want to know if a man by the name of Henry Fisher used one of your computers on March 20th and again on March 29th."

"That's it?"

"Yes."

"Just a moment," she said.

She left the room coming back a few minutes later. "Yes, he was here on both those dates."

"Do you know what time of day?"

"Both visits were at twelve noon. Does that help?"

"Definitely. How long will that information be kept in your computer?"

"We don't clear it. We always have a record of what our members borrow, be it books or time on one of our computers."

"We may need you to testify in court at some point."

"Not a problem. Happy to help law enforcement."

Both detectives thanked the woman before making their way back to their vehicle.

"We now know how Castle found out the judge's dirty secret, but we can't prove it, can we?" Walters said.

"Perhaps not, but it's pretty clear they saw each other in the library. Castle was walking by and saw the husband of his female law partner, Constance Carroll, and in wanting to say hello he no doubt saw what was on the judge's screen. Castle didn't confide in his wife about the encounter, at least she claims. Would he have confided in one of his other partners? That would make sense, wouldn't it?"

"Definitely."

Josh Sutton called Murray Castle's law firm and asked to speak with Gabriel Mercer's assistant. Once she was on the line, he asked her if her boss was in the office. She said yes. Did he have an appointment in the next hour or so? She replied no.

"Very well," Sutton said. "Please tell him that detectives Sutton is on his way and wishes to talk to him."

When Sutton and Walters were seated across the desk from Mercer, Sutton asked the lawyer if Murray Castle confided in him when something was bothering him.

"We were partners, so we talked often. We discussed our cases and tried to help each other."

"I understand that. What we want to know is if Murray Castle talked to you about things not related to his work?"

"I suppose. I mean we both liked hockey and often discussed games, for example. Is that what you mean?"

"Let me be clear. Did Mr. Castle discuss his having seen a judge, totally by accident, under somewhat unusual circumstances?"

"Not that I recall," Mercer said pleasantly, but Sutton had caught the slight hesitation before the reply.

"You told me that Murray Castle was your friend and that you wanted us to find his killer. One way is for you to be honest," Sutton said. "He did discuss a judge, did he not?"

"Briefly, but that's it. He started to talk about seeing a judge in a library, but then stopped. I guess he changed his mind about telling me what happened."

"Did he tell you the name of the judge?" Walters asked.

"No, he did not. And that's the truth. I asked him about it the next day or a couple of days later, but he said he'd made a mistake and to forget it, which I did. Are you saying that Murray's killer could be a judge? That would be ... insane. Why would a judge want to kill Murray? Because of the nature of his work he never argued cases in court. I don't believe he dealt with a judge in all the years he was a lawyer."

"We're investigating, Mr. Mercer. That's just one avenue."

"I'd appreciate it if you could keep me informed."

"We'll do our best," Walters promised.

As the two detectives were on their way back to the division, Walters asked Sutton what his thoughts were.

"I think Mercer is telling the truth. The way I see it, Castle didn't think it was appropriate to talk to Mercer, but I wonder if he could have approached the judge's wife, Constance Carroll," Sutton offered. "Probably not. It would certainly have been rather awkward."

"Castle may have gone to speak to both of them in their condo. I mean that would make sense. What do you think?" Walters asked.

"I wonder. I'm sure he didn't know whether or not Carroll was aware of her husband's hobby so he would have tried to spare her. From the way people talk about Castle, he was conscientious. He tried to save his client Lacrosse some money although it got him into legal trouble. As Dr. Castle paints her husband, he most probably tried to put some sense into the judge, push him toward getting help. Of course, as we now know the judge was not ready to mend his ways."

"Could be, but we'll never know if that happened, will we?" Walters asked.

"You know, in the hope of helping the judge, even if it proved awkward, Castle could have approached Constance Carroll. Of course she would have been terribly insulted that someone would think her distinguished husband was a paedophile. It might be worth considering that she might be the one who decided Castle had to go, then had a poisoned pill made. Once she had the pill it was easy for her to put it in

Castle's pillbox without the judge knowing anything about it. Whether her husband was aware of it or not, she may be the one who killed her law partner."

"Certainly looks like it, but we can't prove it," Walters concluded.

"There's always tomorrow," Sutton added. "And I was thinking that we know little about judge Evers. We need to find out more about his life outside of paedophilia."

"I can look into that. My ten-year-old twin nieces go to a camp each summer. I want to know more about the judge's involvement in children's camps to make sure my sister's girls are not in danger from people like Evers."

"Great. Go for it. We'll talk next week. Anna and I are getting away this weekend."

"Good for you. Where're you going?"

"Not far, just Niagara. It's still not tourist season at the falls so it should be a perfect time to go."

CHAPTER THIRTY-FOUR

After checking in their hotel, Anna and Josh Sutton walked hand in hand as they made their way to the promenade along the Niagara River offering an amazing view of both the Canadian and American falls. Despite the cool weather many tourists had found their way to the legendary area. They, like Anna and Josh, were close enough to feel some of the water droplets carried by the wind as the water from the Upper Niagara River shot down the falls at the Canadian horseshoe escarpment to the Lower Niagara River at a rate of more than six-hundred-and-eighty-thousand gallons per second.

"This place still amazes me," Anna said. "And I still remember our first visit here. You were trying to impress me."

He smiled. "No doubt about that. I was crazy in love with you and I kept hoping you felt the same."

"You know I did," she said as she wiped large drops of water from her face only to realize it was raining when Josh did the same.

They both laughed.

"I suppose we should get back."

They ate lunch in a restaurant in their hotel. As the waiter was serving their plates of Caesar salads, Josh recognized the tall man who was walking in and making his way to a table.

"Someone you know?" Anna asked.

"Yeah. He's a prof at the U of T. His name's Blanchard."

As Josh and Anna ate slowly, the detective saw that Blanchard gulped down a sandwich then quickly left the restaurant.

"What should we do after lunch?" Anna asked. "I see it's still raining so going for a walk is out of the question. We can check out the casino without having to go outside."

"Why not? Last time we didn't."

A bit later they were walking through the main room of the casino and taking it all in. Josh wondered how some people could think that gambling was fun. Then he saw Blanchard at a black jack table engrossed in the activity in front of him. Josh saw that the minimum wage at that table was one hundred dollars. He and Anna watched the action long enough to see that Blanchard was losing. They continued their recon walk.

When they saw a row of slots, Anna retrieved a loonie from her purse and tried her luck at a machine just vacated by an older woman. She pushed the button and, after a moment when a set of spinning symbols were activated, three cherries lined up. A light went on above the gambling machine and dollars loudly poured out into the lower receptacle for what, to Anna, seemed several minutes when in fact it was only twenty seconds. She laughed a hefty laugh which made Josh chuckle.

A beefy man approached. "Congratulations," he told Anna. "You got over hundred dollars," and he handed her a cardboard container with the casino's logo. "The cashier'll be happy to exchange these for paper money when you're ready."

She thanked him, and began scooping up the large coins.

"Things are looking up," Josh told her as he helped.

As they walked away from the slots section an idea which had been forming in Sutton's mind needed clarification. "Would you mind being by yourself for a few minutes? I want to check out something. About work."

"Sure," Anna said, fully aware that the minds of detectives were always on call. "I wanted to get some magazines downstairs anyway. I'll get paper for these loonies and meet you in the lobby when you're done."

He kissed her realizing, as he often did, that she was truly the better half of himself.

Sutton looked around the casino and saw that the beefy man walking around, keeping an eye on the gambling tables that attracted high rollers. *Him for sure*, Sutton thought as he approached.

"Excuse me," he said to the man, "can you tell me where I could find the manager of the casino?"

"Right here," the man said, pointing to himself.

"Good." Discreetly, Sutton showed his badge to the man. "I'm a major crime detective in Toronto—"

"Everything's above board in our casinos. After all we're governed by the Ontario lottery."

Surprised by the remark, Sutton frowned briefly. "I don't want to investigate your operation. I'm here for a weekend of R&R with my wife but I saw a man at one of your tables that could be of interest in one of our investigations. I'd like to know if you know anything about him."

"Happy to help," the man said with a sudden crooked smile.

"He's at the one-hundred-dollar blackjack table over there," Josh said, pointing. "The tall gentleman wearing the blue shirt."

"You mean Joe Blanchard?"

"You know him then?"

"I suppose you could say I know his gambling habits. Not much else except that he's a doctor."

"Does he come in here often?"

"Funny thing. He used to come in all the time but stopped after ... "

Sutton waited.

"One day he asked for credit. I refused of course. We're not Las Vegas where high rollers are cultivated. I didn't see him again for a while."

"I take it he lost money."

"All gamblers end up losing money. It's the nature of the beast. Of course they think it won't happen to them."

"When did he come back?"

"A couple weeks ago. Maybe three. Seems to have all the money he needs now."

"Appreciate your input. It could be very useful."

"Happy to help," the man repeated.

When Josh Sutton joined his wife in the lobby she had a few magazines on her lap and was staring straight ahead. When he approached he saw that her eyes were full of tears.

He sat beside her and put an arm around her shoulders. "Honey…"

She put her head on his chest. "You know, I wish I could forget what happened to Bryan like I did before."

"Do you really want to do that? It's much better to remember that we were blessed with a sweet boy for many years."

"I know it was a privilege to be his mom, but why did he have to leave us?"

"The Universe made the decision for a reason even if we don't know that reason. But we'll always remember how wonderful he was. You know, the pandemic made lots of victims, not just us. We're only one family among the many who are still grieving."

She lifted her head back up and blew her nose.

"I read online the other day that there are various groups that offer meetings for those who lost someone to the pandemic," he said. "It might be good for us to grieve with others who are in the same boat. What do you think?"

"I suppose we could do that."

By the time the Suttons got back home on Sunday, the sky was clear blue, and both felt renewed after spending time grieving the past and examining the possibilities of the future.

"We should do this more often," Josh told Anna as they entered their house. "Let's look at where we could go this summer. My current big case should be wrapped up by then."

CHAPTER THIRTY-FIVE

It was after lunch the next day when Sutton and Walters got together to compare notes and recap their progress. Walters spoke first.

"I looked at everything I could find on Evers. Officially, he's well respected as a judge of the Ontario Superior Court for being fair. He's been married to Constance Carroll for twenty-five years with no children. They live in a high-end condo in the northern section of the city as you know. They are involved in the financing of two summer camps for children in the Kawartha region near Peterborough. That's it. As far as I could find out they finance but they don't visit the camps. Because of the couple's monetary involvement the name of Carroll's law firm is front and centre online and in the publicity literature for both camps. That's all I could dig up."

"You're sure the judge doesn't visit the camps?"

"Oh, yeah. I checked that in as many ways as I could. I was able to talk to the directors of both camps who assured me the judge has never been to either camp."

"So, as I see it," Sutton said, "he filmed his disgusting videos somewhere else. But where?"

"You know," Walters began, "when I was talking to my contact in London, he told me that they found out that many of the disgusting videos are filmed in poor countries. The kids are lured by the money they get."

"I guess that's one way of avoiding Canadian laws," Sutton commented.

"It's depressing that we can't prove he uploaded videos. All we know is that he used a fake name to access child porn sites. However," Walters added, "through London we can prove that he chatted with others and was not just looking, like Norbert Perkins."

"That's something, but we can't link him to Castle's murder just yet, although I found out something interesting during my visit to the falls."

"Do tell."

Sutton apprised his colleague on seeing Joe Blanchard in a casino and what he had learned from the manager. "It looks like the good doctor suddenly came into money a few weeks ago. Perhaps money for making an aconite pill, question mark? It's a possibility we have to examine closely. There is no doubt that he has the knowledge and the training for making such a pill. But how do we prove that he got money from either the judge or his wife?"

"Through bank accounts," Walters offered.

"I dug into those this morning, but didn't find out anything. No large withdrawals or deposits in any account. As far as Blanchard is concerned, he has a few hundred dollars in his savings account while his checking account is almost always overdrawn although he has a good income from the lab where he works as well at the U of T. I could not find any other account in another bank. He was married to one Susan Lowell, they were divorced three years ago. They have one son. The good doctor pays alimony and child support. And gambles. It has to make quite a dent in his revenue.

"As for the power couple they could have out-of-the-country accounts like in Florida, for example, if they go down there in winter as many Canadians do. And then Blanchard could have insisted on cash. I mean he knew the pill was dangerous, and while he may be a doctor who took an oath to do no harm, his secret passion for gambling was no doubt desperately calling. Digging into U.S. bank accounts can be somewhat more complicated than digging into Canadian ones, but I'm all set on going that route."

"While you're doing that, I'll check into the judge's credit card charges. If they took a long trip out of the country in the last few years, they certainly charged it to a card."

As Sutton went back to online investigation, one thing was not clear in his mind. If his theory was bang on, how did Constance Carroll and Joe Blanchard meet? And how did she know he could make a poisoned pill? The detective was well aware that every day brought out a new set of questions that needed more investigation and answers.

He picked up his desk phone and called Cecilia at Castle's firm.

She seemed glad to hear from the detective. "What can I do for you today?"

"I assume Mrs. Carroll has her own assistant?"

"Yes, she does. Judy is her name, but she's away on compassionate leave right now because her husband is terribly ill and not expected to live much more than a few days."

"Sorry to hear. Then, who works for Mrs. Carroll?"

"She works with a paralegal, of course, and a temp assistant is supposed to be hired when Mrs. Carroll returns."

"I see. So, if I wanted to verify some of her cases, could the paralegal give me the information?"

"I suppose so. But I also could if I asked Mr. Mercer's permission."

"That's fine. In fact, welcome. I could call him if you want," Sutton offered.

"Let me talk to him. What exactly are you looking for?"

Sutton told Cecilia that he wanted to know if Constance Carroll had been involved in a case with or about the U of T, as well as one related to the lab where Blanchard worked. "I don't want any details relative to the cases," Sutton said. "I just want to verify that she did or does work for either or both of these institutions. That's it."

"I'll get back to you as soon as I can."

Walters was digging into judge Harold Evers past calendar on the bench. He saw that when the pandemic was at its height in Canada and the rest of the world some of the court cases in Ontario had been postponed. At first, judge Evers and most of the other magistrates had little duty until cases began to be heard with the help of modern communication devices. The lawyers appeared via video to present their arguments. As far as Walters could ascertain, it had all worked very well until courts were finally allowed to reopen to hear cases in person.

The lull in the work of judges had been a good time for them to travel, Walters thought, except that airlines had been basically grounded as people feared air travel. As well, the southern Canadian border was shut tight making it impossible to travel to the U.S.

The detective nevertheless began looking into the judge's credit card charges for the period since the pandemic ended. Comparing his spending in that period with those during the pandemic and the twelve months pre-pandemic, Walters saw little difference. However when he continued digging he saw that, nearly two years before the pandemic invaded the world, the judge had charged an Air Canada flight to one of his credit cards. With some more work the detective was able to determine that it had been a return flight from Toronto to Prague, Czech Republic, for himself and a person named C. Evers. The trip had lasted a week.

A brother? A cousin? Or, of course, his wife if she uses her married name for official records like a passport or tax returns, Walters considered.

The detective then mused that he had recently read online that Prague was reputed as a beautiful city and that its people were also especially beautiful. A good place to go to shoot videos of children. But with his wife along?

So many questions, so few answers the detective thought.

CHAPTER THIRTY-SIX

Josh Sutton felt frustrated after his efforts to get information on possible U.S. bank accounts belonging to judge Evers went nowhere. Despite getting the cooperation of American law enforcement personnel it had been a colossal dead end.

But relying on his guts, as he often did, the detective dug further into Canadian records and found that the judge had an American currency bank account in a local bank other than the one where his regular checking and savings accounts were held. There was only a little over two thousand dollars in the account, and he saw that it was seldom used. The last time was nearly a year earlier when a small deposit had been made online. Sutton assumed that the money was accessed to cover cash expenses and purchases when the judge drove south of the border since there was a branch of the bank close to the courthouse.

Sutton knew his dad had such an account he used when he needed an auto part he couldn't get quickly in Canada. Because he bought U.S. currency when the exchange rate was acceptable, it saved money when the rate was ridiculously high.

U.S. currency bank accounts were offered by all banks in Canada. It certainly did not indicate anything nefarious on the part of the judge.

But what about Constance Carroll? Sutton did not find any U.S. currency account under that name, but he did find an account for C.

Evers at a bank branch on the first floor of her office building. Convenient, Sutton thought, as he uncovered that the balance of the account was almost nil following a withdrawal of ten thousand dollars a few weeks earlier.

Eureka, Sutton sang to himself.

The detective's thoughts were interrupted by his ringing phone, and he was pleased that Cecilia was on the other end of the line.

"Detective, Mr. Mercer urged me to cooperate with you as much as I could. I looked into Mrs. Carroll's records and found something that could be related to the information you wanted. The name of the lab you gave me is on Mrs. Carroll's calendar. Her notes indicate that she went there about three weeks ago, and from what I could gather it was to assess the lab before taking on a possible new client. Does that help?"

"Yes, very much. Thank you for giving us a hand."

"Happy to do it, detective."

Sutton and Walters spent some time apprising their captain of the details of their investigation. They ended by pointing out that it was not possible to charge either the judge or his wife with murder or conspiracy to commit murder as they were not able to get the proof they needed.

"We know the judge's wife visited a lab where Dr. Blanchard works and that he had the knowledge and opportunity to make a poisoned pill, but it was certainly made on the sly so a warrant to examine the premises would surely be useless," Sutton said. "We are certain that she paid Blanchard to make the poisoned pill with cash she withdrew from her U.S. currency account, but we can't prove it. Blanchard did not make any deposits into his own bank account. He might have hidden the cash under his mattress for all we know."

As for the charge of paedophilia against the judge, Walters explained that it would come from London through official channels when the British were ready to go public with their case.

Captain Corbett listened closely and told the detectives he was very proud of all their efforts, adding that all was not lost.

"At this point, it would be wise to get pre-charge advice from the crown attorney. I mean everyone wants to make sure that when the necessary proof is gathered the pair is effectively prosecuted. That means that any problems should then be dealt with efficiency before the charges are laid," the captain said. "And another thing is that in consultation with the crown you will be able to build an air-tight case. That has to be priority one because it's certain that the defence for both the judge and his wife will scrutinize the details of the prosecution's case with a fine toothcomb. They'll work diligently to uncover the most minute slip-up."

CHAPTER THIRTY-SEVEN

Prior to a possible meeting with a crown attorney, Sutton was convinced that talking to Constance Carroll was warranted. He and Walters made their way to the distinctive condo building and rang the unit in question.

At the voice of Carroll asking who was at the door, Sutton identified himself although that was not necessary because of the camera relaying a visual of the detective in the condo unit.

"What exactly do you want?" she asked in a somewhat harsh tone.

"We would like to ask you a few questions relative to the murder of Murray Castle."

"I don't know anything more than what I've already told you."

"Our investigation has taken us into a new area and your input could be useful."

No reply was heard for several seconds until she said: "Okay, but you better make it quick."

The buzzer unlocked the lobby door and the two detectives made their way to the elevators.

Constance Carroll's face still showed signs of facial surgery, although Sutton thought that healing was well on the way. She invited them to sit in the roomy mostly white living area.

"So, what exactly do you need, detective?" she asked as she herself sat.

"Our investigation has led us to a lab that does a lot of work for the government, the one that was credited for finding one of the effective vaccines that was instrumental in stopping covid in its track. We understand that you visited the lab and we'd like to know what you know about it."

She hesitated a moment. "I don't know anything about it. I mean I was approached by a possible client who is set on suing the lab. He believes that lab personnel stole and profited from some of his research. That's it. I simply went there to see the installation for myself before committing my time to the litigation."

"I imagine someone gave you a guided tour."

"Yes. I wanted to see for myself how they work."

Walters spoke: "Was your guide Dr. Blanchard?"

"Of course. I had contacted him in advance," she replied. The comment surprised the detectives for a moment, until she added: "As you surely know, he was married to my niece Susan, so I know him. Why are you asking about Joe? He's certainly not involved in Murray's murder!"

The remark was a classic one, Sutton thought. Dive right into the fray to divert suspicion. Or at least, attempt to. "That's what we're trying to find out."

"Why would Joe kill one of my law partners? I'm certain he didn't even know Murray."

"Are you quite sure?" Walters asked.

"Well, I can't swear to it, but I'm sure Murray never met anyone in my family so how would he have known Joe? They worked in totally different fields."

"Perhaps a chance meeting. We will be checking it out," Sutton offered, then tried a different topic. "Ms. Carroll, do you ever go by your married name?"

"Yes, like many other women, depending on the circumstances. For example, my passport is in my married name because it's simpler when I travel with my husband. Also for income tax purposes, it's advantageous. Why do you ask?"

"Just curious," Sutton said.

"Both names are perfectly legal."

"Certainly. Well, that's all for now. Thank you for your time. We'll get back to you if we need more details."

Back in their vehicle, both detectives were assessing the encounter with the lawyer.

"When I investigated the judge earlier, I also took a peak at his wife. Her clients all seem to be pleased with her work on their behalf if I go by comments online," Walters said.

"What's your point?"

"She seems nice and stands for justice in court. Are we sure she iced her law partner after premeditating every last complicated steps leading to his murder?" Walters asked, not sure if an answer would be forthcoming.

"Like Anna's therapist said, it's impossible to predict who is capable of murder. Even those seen as nice people do murder. The first time I saw Carroll I was very surprised that she didn't react when I told her Castle had been murdered. I thought it was odd for a woman to show no emotion to a murder. Now I know, in fact I'm certain, it's because she had done the nasty deed.

"The way I see it, both the judge and his wife have built exemplary careers and reputations over the years. They have no children to distract them from themselves and from keeping up their status in the community. One way or another Constance Carroll found out about Murray Castle trying to help her husband see the error of his ways. Castle could have contacted her directly about the problem, but of course we'll never know.

"She may or may not have known about the judge's paedophilia until Castle told her, or she may have known, but one way or another she wasn't about to let her partner tell the world about her husband's secret. She probably didn't see any other way out than murder and went searching for the perfect method that wouldn't leave a trace. Once she had determined how she would kill Castle, she knew exactly where to go to get the poisoned pill. Of course, she was convinced there wouldn't be an autopsy."

"How can we prove she hired the good doctor to make a poisoned pill? Right now that seems impossible to me," Walters offered.

"I'm sure there's a way. We just got to find it," Sutton said. "Let's start by concentrating on Blanchard."

"As you said getting a warrant to search the lab would probably be a waste of time, but what if the doctor worked on the pill at home?"

"It seems to me he'd need some sort of equipment like what's used by manufacturers of vitamin tablets. I mean it's not just a question of compacting aconite. The mixture must have had to be compressed and hardened in some way so it'd look like a vitamin pill."

"You're right. Can we get a warrant for his home?"

"At this point, it's the only way to go."

Sutton and Walters were at a meeting with the provincial attorney general, grey-haired and stern-faced Michael Perron, and a tall assistant attorney by the name of Angie. Although the detectives had introduced their investigative results, the lead crown prosecutor still could not believe that a judge of the superior court of the province was a sick individual who visited child porn sites and could possibly have been in cahoots with his wife, a reputed barrister, to kill a lawyer. It was just too incredible.

"Captain Corbett suggested that all of us cooperate to make certain the final phase of the investigation into the murder of Murray Castle ensures that the formal charges lead to convictions. As you are aware the paedophilia charges will come from London through proper channels in due course," Sutton said.

Perron asked the detectives what they planned as their next steps.

Sutton spoke. "We know that Constance Carroll and Dr. Joe Blanchard are related by marriage and know each other reasonably well. In deciding to kill Castle, she had to know that Blanchard could make a poisoned pill. For a price. She had to know he's a gambler because it could have been the reason her niece divorced him. That means that money would be a welcome incentive for the doctor. The question is how to prove it. She took money out of her account but he never made any bank deposits as far as we could determine. We wonder if having both of them trailed could be the way to go?"

"Hum," Perron uttered. "It'd probably be a waste of time."

"Perhaps. We've asked for a warrant for Blanchard's home and are waiting for it."

"What exactly are you hoping to find?"

"Some proof that he made a poisoned tablet for Constance Carroll. Perhaps equipment that would have been required for the deed, or some sort of aconite stash."

"Hum. Interesting," Perron commented. "If he has such things in his home that would mean that he had no idea that the pill he made would be used for a murder, don't you think? Otherwise he would have gotten rid of any trace of his activities."

"Good point," Sutton said. "But he might never have considered that the police would connect him to his wife's aunt."

"True. In any event, I hope your search will be successful."

CHAPTER THIRTY-EIGHT

Sutton and Walters had decided that the element of surprise was their only viable option. They waited for Blanchard in front of his condo building knowing that he lived in a small unit on the first floor. The building, on the western fringe of downtown, was definitely vintage, but seemed to be reasonably well kept.

They saw Blanchard walking toward his building just after six thirty, carrying what appeared to be take-out food. The tall man had an air of assuredness about him which, for Sutton, possibly confirmed Dr. Maxwell's theory that murderers did not telegraph their ugly deeds.

They waited some fifteen minutes before making their move to give Blanchard time to eat. As they approached the front door, a couple unlocked it and, no doubt thinking the two men also lived in the building, held the door open for the detectives who thanked them with smiles. The couple went for the elevators while the detectives casually walked down the first floor corridor. As the couple disappeared inside an elevator Sutton was knocking on Blanchard's door.

The door opened quickly and the good doctor was clearly surprised. After a momentary hesitation he said: "You're the detective who contacted me at the university. I remember you."

"Good," Sutton said. "Then you know why we have a warrant to search your home."

Walters took it out of his inside jacket pocket and handed it to a seemingly baffled Blanchard who took it and quickly scanned it. He then invited the two men inside with a sweep of his hand.

"What exactly are you looking for, may I ask?"

"For proof that you were an accessory to murder," Sutton replied.

"What the hell are you talking about? I'm not a murderer."

"We'll see, won't we?"

At first glance the unit appeared neat but it was sparsely furnished. The detectives put on gloves and made their way toward the two bedrooms at the back as Blanchard sat on the grey sofa, crossing his legs, appearing quite undisturbed. Neither the main bedroom nor the smaller one showed any sign of anything closely related to the preparation of poisons once the two men had looked into every drawer, every nook and cranny, every closet and even every pocket. The smaller bedroom was clearly used by Blanchard's son during his visits, but that did not deter the detectives from examining it thoroughly.

A painstaking search of the bathroom's various shelves and storage spaces did not reveal anything related to their mandate. The only medicine Blanchard had in his bathroom was a bottle of painkillers.

The two men walked back to the living room.

"I take it you didn't find what you were looking for because there is nothing to find," Blanchard explained forcefully.

"We're not quite done," Sutton replied, and the men set out to examine the kitchen. There was a dirty mug and a used glass in the sink, but the counters were free of clutter except for a microwave, a toaster and a single-cup coffee maker. The detectives looked into all the cupboards and all the drawers. Sutton did not see the need to empty food containers like cereal boxes to look for the pills which, he was quite certain, would not be in close contact with food. Everything indicated a kitchen like any other kitchen.

They then moved to the refrigerator where they found nothing but food. When they opened the freezer door they saw that it was rather packed, but that did not deter them from taking the packages out and putting them on a counter.

Blanchard quickly appeared. "What do you think you're doing? This food will spoil."

"Not to worry. We won't be long," Walters said. "Please go sit and let us do what we came to do."

The doctor went to sit on one of the chairs around the dining table from where he could watch the action in the kitchen. That alerted the detective to be extra careful.

There were eight frozen prepared meals ready to pop into the microwave for easy and quick dinners. The perfect solution for a man living alone and with his son one day a week. In addition, there was a loaf of bread, a large container of chocolate ice cream and a few bags of frozen berries.

Because Blanchard continued to keep boring into what they were doing Sutton was convinced that they were indeed on the right track. They had not found equipment of any kind that could have been used in making poisoned pills in the condo, but the good doctor could have made them at the lab on the sly. And he could have made extra pills that he brought home and kept in his freezer for possible future use.

Suddenly, Sutton realized that that could not be the case. While Anna was at Montrose and their home freezer was not inventoried regularly as she used to do, he often found that food inside the bags in the freezer was covered with snow-like ice. While he knew little about poisons, he considered that aconite pills would no doubt suffer from being kept inside a bag in a freezer. They had to look elsewhere.

He signalled to Walters and they carefully put all the items they had taken out of the freezer back as they had found them. Then Sutton realized that no matter his secrets Blanchard would protect his son and would have hidden any extra pills in something where his son was not likely to look. The boy was nine so a coffeemaker was a safe bet.

Beside the one-cup coffeemaker on the corner of the main counter there was a cylindrical container, and Sutton judged that it held more than a dozen small pods ready to fulfil the doctor's need for caffeine. He slowly emptied the container on the counter. Pods poured out along with a small caramel-coloured plastic container with two small round pink pills inside. Both detectives turned to look at Blanchard who was now immobile and staring at the floor.

Sutton put the small container into an evidence bag he got from one of his pockets before approaching the doctor. Walters took time to put the pods back into their container.

"Dr. Blanchard," Sutton said, "we need to talk to you about these tablets. Please come with us.

CHAPTER THIRTY-NINE

Dr. Joe Blanchard was sitting alone at the table in an interrogation room featuring a mirrored glass wall. He knew that on the other side of the mirror he was being not only watched but that his movements and facial expressions were being closely monitored and analyzed.

Michael Perron, the chief crown prosecutor, had joined Captain Corbett and Ross Walters behind the glass. Josh Sutton entered the interrogation room.

"Dr. Blanchard, our forensic lab has determined that the pills that we found with your coffee pods are aconite tablets and, as you know, a concentrated form of poison. Why were they in your home?"

"They were the end result of an experiment on poisons that I conducted in the lab where I work."

"Really? Why would you have taken them home? A very dangerous move since your young son visits you regularly."

"That's why I kept them with my coffee. He'd never look there for anything."

"But why were you hanging on to something that dangerous?"

"Aconite is dangerous if you don't know how to use it."

"These particular tablets could stop a heart in an instant. You know that. We know that. Just like they stopped Murray Castle's heart."

"Who?"

"Come on, doctor. The man you conspired to kill. How much did you get to help murder a caring husband and father? Enough so you can continue to gamble your life away?"

"What are talking about? I never killed anyone. I'm a physician who does research to save lives, I do not murder people."

"Then why did your wife's aunt withdraw a large sum of money recently?"

"First of all, it's my ex-wife. Second, how do I know what her aunt does with her money."

"You did show her around your lab, did you not?"

"She was working on a case of someone suing the lab and she wanted to see it for herself. She knew I worked there, so she asked if I could be assigned to show her around."

"But you did supply Ms. Carroll with a poisoned tablet while she was in your lab."

"No, I did not."

"If the lady talks first, you'll be up a creek without a paddle, as the saying goes."

"At the risk of repeating myself, I have no idea what you're talking about. Her visit to the lab concerned a civil case she's handling or thinking of taking on, not quite sure which. That's it. I want to leave now, I'm teaching a class in the morning."

Sutton said. "Your partner in crime will sell you out in an instant."

"My partner in crime? Why in hell would I conspire with Connie on anything? I don't even know her very well. I say enough," Blanchard said forcefully. "I've answered your questions. That's it." He stood up and the detective knew he could not hold him.

"We'll talk again," the detective promised. "Soon."

Gathered around a table with coffees, the law enforcement people were in full discussion mood.

Sutton spoke. "I'm thinking that he might never have known that his aunt-in-law was going to kill someone. Let me rephrase that. She offered him a lot of money, enough to feed his gambling habit for some time so he probably convinced himself that she'd never hurt anyone with the pill he gave her."

"Then why would she need poison if not to kill someone?" Perron asked.

"She probably told him some elaborate yarn about a case she was handling that Blanchard didn't care to examine too closely because he was blinded by the money he'd get."

"So, what now? Can we charge him with conspiracy to commit murder?" Walters asked.

"I don't see how," Perron said. "You're sure there was only one call from the lawyer to Blanchard?"

"Very sure."

"Then you need to shake the lady down."

As soon as the officer charged with driving him back home stopped in front of his condo building, Blanchard quickly got out and almost sprinted to the front door. Once inside, as he was walking down the corridor to his unit, his phone connected him with Constance Carroll who was getting ready for bed.

"What's up, Joe? It's late."

"I've just come back from being interrogated by the police. Connie, what did you use those three pills for?"

"I told you. It was for a case."

"What case? Anything to do with your partner, Castle?"

"Come on. I'd never murder anyone. Why were they questioning you, anyway?"

"They knew you came to the lab and think that I supplied the pills then."

"What did you tell them?"

"Nothing. Was there something to tell?" Blanchard asked.

"Of course not. You worry too much. The police are just looking at everyone in our office because of my partner's murder hoping to catch someone. That's all. They're just fishing."

But Blanchard didn't believe her. He figured they were investigating her through him and realized that he should have been more firm in his refusal to supply the tablets when she first came to see him at home. That week he was working on making pills using various materials to see which ones were easier to form into tablets, and he had included aconite as one possibility to perhaps mix with other elements because of its malleability. Carroll had told him that she was seeking a poisoned pill that looked like a vitamin tablet to present in court for a case she was handling. She said the client would pay him for his trouble but when he refused she told him that without it she would certainly lose her case and a lot of money.

The good doctor had not wanted to supply the tablets but it was his nature to help people. Besides she kept anteing the pot. When it reached ten grand he decided that because she was a lawyer she would only use the pills to boost her case in front of a jury. It had been easy. He had already fashioned a few aconite tablets which could serve her purpose because of their colour. He had packaged three in a padded envelope which he mailed to her office, marked personal and confidential. The police would not be able to trace that.

He also knew that when they investigated his phone calls there was only one call from Constance Carroll's office to his phone. Nothing to raise questions. She had gone to the trouble of coming to talk to him in person at home more than once to press him to give her the tablets she wanted. Could she then have been carefully planning all her movements in case of a police investigation? Pretty cold, Blanchard thought, but he still didn't think she could murder anyone.

The detective who interrogated him did not press the question of why the poisoned pills were in his home. If asked, Blanchard was not sure how he'd have replied. Yet, he knew why he had done it in the first place: he wanted to be ready if more tablets were needed and the price was again interesting.

The money had been very welcome, especially since his ex was starting to make waves because he was behind in his financial obligation to her. He was now up to date in his payments and the rest of the money was very secure in a bank deposit box. He again praised himself for not depositing it in a bank which the police would have found.

While he himself was getting ready for bed, he knew he had to do something about his gambling if he wanted to keep the rest of the money and start saving instead of spending. Tomorrow he would contact the man who had offered twice to help him lose his taste for gambling.

When he turned off his bedside lamp he knew it was quite clear that if he had said no to Connie Carroll he would not be on the police radar. Yet while the thought kept appearing in his mind he simply couldn't believe that she was capable of murder. Perhaps her comment was right on. The police were simply scrutinizing the people in her office.

He was soon asleep.

Constance Carroll closely examined her face in the mirror in her bathroom. Not too bad, she thought. There was still discoloration, but when she went back to work in a few days, some good foundation would ensure that all signs of surgery had vanished. She had to look her best in front of her colleagues and in the courtroom, however right now she had to concentrate on remaining calm despite Joe Blanchard's questions. Quickly, she decided that she'd forget about all that tonight. She needed her beauty sleep.

She suspected her husband the judge was probably asleep in front of the television as happened often these days. She made her way to the den and, sure enough, he was slouched in his favourite easy chair. Taking the remote from the table next to his elbow, she turned off the large set.

"Harry," she began. "Wake up. Let's go to bed."

When he didn't move at all, she shook his shoulder. "Harry, wake up, dear," she said but he did not move. She tried a second time, this time noticing that his lips were bluish. "Harry," she cried putting her fingers around his wrist. There was a pulse, but it was very weak.

In a moment she was giving the address of her condo building to the 911 operator, insisting on speed.

Josh Sutton and Ross Walters were trying to decide how to best approach Constance Carroll when they saw Captain Corbett coming towards them.

"Gentlemen," he said. "Your investigation just took an unexpected turn. I've just been informed that judge Harold Evers underwent emergency cardiac surgery during the night. He's now in intensive care at the TGH. I'm told his wife is with him."

"Doctors would have known if he had ingested aconite, wouldn't they?" Sutton asked.

"You think that she'd be capable of killing her husband?"

"I wouldn't put it past her."

"But, if she had given him one of those pills, he'd be dead."

"Yeah. I suppose so."

"Well, going after her today is certainly out of the question."

After Corbett had left, Walters commented that they certainly had enough other tasks awaiting their attention to keep them busy for a few days.

CHAPTER FORTY

Constance Carroll Evers was looking at her husband behind the ICU glass of the cardiac centre at the Toronto General Hospital. He looked asleep while an array of humming machines showed measurements and numbers of various types. She was wondering if he would survive when their family physician approached.

The woman was a nearly sixty-year-old with short grey hair and a no-nonsense approach to life. She liked to be called Dr. Joan. "I had warned him that he needed to have his heart examined. I gave him a referral to the best cardiac doctor in Toronto, but your stubborn husband ignored it all. Was too busy," she said while shaking her head. "I'll never understand why some people feel that work is more important than their health."

The lawyer blew a breath. "He first wanted to clear the backlog of cases still pending before the courts because of the pandemic. Is he going to make it?"

"I just looked at the surgeon's notes; your judge will no doubt be up and around in no time. Meanwhile, how are you doing? You should be home resting. Staying here, looking at him sleep, is not helpful."

"I know, but I like to think that by sending him positive thoughts I'm helping him heal. I don't know what I would do if he died."

"He's not the first man to have heart surgery. He'll be fine and back home before you know it. That's where you should be; home and resting. The hospital will contact you if there's a change. Do you want me to prescribe something to help you sleep?"

"Appreciated, but no. I'll be okay."

Back in her condo unit, Constance simply collapsed on her side of the bed. Before she could examine her situation, the exhaustion took over and in a moment she was asleep. The buzzing of her phone woke her more than two hours later. It was Gabriel Mercer.

"Connie, I hope I'm not calling at a bad time. How is he and how are you?"

"Both as well as can be expected. They tell me he's going to be fine, but that it's going to take a while."

"Of course. Is there anything I can do?"

"Thanks, Gabe, but there's nothing to do. I was planning to go back to work on Monday, but I may delay. I'll have to see how things go."

"Take all the time you need."

After the call ended she took a long hot shower which made her feel marginally better. After drying herself and wrapping her body in a thick terrycloth robe she made her way to the kitchen for something to eat. She decided on popping a prepared curry dish into the microwave and make herself a cup of green tea. When everything was ready she went to eat in front of the television. She needed to concentrate on something other than the reality she was now facing.

But she was unable to focus on the comedy on the screen in front of her because her mind was in a full reminiscing mood now that the love of her life, her soul mate, was fighting to stay alive. She was remembering how she first met Harold the summer after her first year in law school. One day she had driven to the Bancroft area of Ontario to visit an aunt and bring back an heirloom quilt her mother had been promised. On the way back, traveling through country roads, she suddenly felt that something was wrong with one of her back tires. She stopped to examine the problem and was distressed to see that the tire was totally flat. She didn't know what to do.

She had never faced a flat before.

She looked around, and saw that there was a farm house a ways from the road, a short walk ahead. Perhaps someone there could help. She picked up her purse and was starting to walk when a young man on a bicycle stopped beside her.

"Having trouble with your car?"

"I've got a flat and don't know how to change a tire."

"Well, I could do it for you. With the right incentive," he said giggling while his curly black hair danced on his head.

He was cute and she immediately decided that he was harmless. "What kind of incentive?"

"A kiss," he replied giggling again.

She giggled herself. "Do all the girls fall for that line?"

"No, but I keep trying. Seriously, I'd be happy to help with the tire."

"I'd appreciate it."

He got off his bike and got busy while young Connie kept her eyes on him. She had a boyfriend in the city, but it was nothing serious as far as she was concerned even if he was a very nice fellow law student. However, the young guy who was now cranking up her car to remove the tire was winning her over with the gorgeous smile he sent her way from time to time.

"Do you live around here?" he asked.

"No. In Toronto. I went to see an aunt in Bancroft."

"I'm glad you did, otherwise I'd never met you."

"What about you? Where do you live?" she asked.

"In the house over there," he said pointing with his chin. "I'm helping my dad with harvesting for a couple of weeks before going back to law school at McGill."

She chuckled.

"What's funny?"

"I also study law but at the U of T."

"Well, well, well. Two future lawyers. What were the chances," he said as he put the damaged tire in her trunk and closed it.

She kissed him quickly on the cheek. He bowed as he thanked her, and asked for her phone number.

"You being in Montreal and me in Toronto is not very practical," she began.

"Studying on the train is just as easy as studying in the library," he argued, and she had to agree.

She had known then that they were made for each other and she had been adoring him ever since. A few years after they were married they built a small house on his parents' farm near the little lazy river that meandered on the edge of the property. Over the years, they had spent as much time in the country as they could. His parents still lived in the main house but hired help did much of the heavy farm work these days.

When Harry was well enough to be released from the hospital, she'd drive him to their hideaway and nurse him back to health.

Murray Castle's efforts to denigrate her husband with his nasty gossip of paedophilia had been an insult and she still had not been able to recover fully. She had told Castle that he was wrong, but he kept insisting that he was certain it was true because he had seen it with his own eyes. The idiot even offered to work with her to get some help for the judge.

The judge was perfect, thank you very much, she had said to herself. Castle was the one who needed help.

And she had helped him to disappear quickly and efficiently, and she was very proud of her direct approach to save her love's reputation. It meant that Castle could never be a danger to either of them ever again.

Now she was certain the police would never catch her. She had been too clever for that nosy detective Sutton. Even if they found out that she had withdrawn a large sum from one of her bank accounts, they had no way of knowing what she used it for because Blanchard had confided he'd keep it in a bank safety deposit box to prevent her niece from ever finding out. She was sure he did just that.

After finishing her meal she explored the bedroom to choose clothes and necessities to bring to the hospital in anticipation of her husband's release. She got a small black bag from his closet and filled it with a casual shirt, some underwear as well as other pieces she felt were appropriate. On opening the top drawer of her husband's chest she came upon his disguises: the light wig he liked, that barely covered the top of his greying curls, along with the matching moustache. He always said they made him feel he was incognito when they went out to a restaurant or a show, or such. He was a judge after all, and didn't want people to berate him in public about any possible grievances relative to his decisions, and she could only agree.

Before finally turning in, she called the hospital and was informed that the judge's condition continued to be stable.

CHAPTER FORTY-ONE

Detective Sutton had decided to keep a distant eye on Constance Carroll. On Sunday morning, while Anna had gone to the mall with her mother who wanted a second opinion about her choice of a dress for the wedding of a friend, he parked his unmarked vehicle across the street from the lawyer's condo building. He was hoping to be able to determine her condition from her countenance. He had called the hospital earlier and had been told that the judge was out of ICU. Good news for him, but not for long. He would no doubt again need specialized care when he learned that his wife was a murderer. Of course, by then, everyone would know he dabbled in child porn.

The orderly and the nurse were satisfied that the patient in their care, one Harold Evers, a middle-aged man who had undergone heart surgery, was now comfortable in the bed in his private room, The orderly checked a second time to make sure the monitor that displayed the patient's heart efforts in the room as well as at the nurses' station was properly plugged into the wall as well as attached to the patient's arm. The judge's had been progressing slowly but surely, and his surgeon had decided he should be moved out of the ICU so that his outlook could be as positive as possible.

The orderly left with the wheelchair that had brought Evers to his new digs while the nurse showed him that she was putting the clothes he had on when he arrived at the hospital in the closet.

"What happened to my other stuff?" he asked.

"Right here," the nurse said, and handed him a small clear plastic bag in which he could see his phone. "We lock all personal items when an unconscious patient gets here, so no one touched anything of yours. The top drawer of your bedside stand locks so your things can be safe while you sleep or are out of the room. Here's the key," she said, handing him a small key on a short chain.

"Thank you very much."

She arranged the call bell so he could easily reach it. "Use this if you need anything," she told him before leaving and closing the door behind her.

After first regaining consciousness he had wondered what had happened to his phone. No doubt Connie had retrieved it and he hoped beyond hope that she didn't look through it although she had never touched his phone. Beside it was password protected and he had never shared it with her.

Despite the fog in his mind after the surgery, he realized that the unexpected happened quickly and that he had to consider making final plans, which meant he had to clear his phone of the pictures that could sully his reputation and offend Connie.

No time like the present, he told himself, and went to work. Over the years he had accumulated dozens of photos on his phone, the ones that he liked best. He argued with himself for a bit about deleting them, however after a while he came to the conclusion that he had to do the right thing, that he had no choice.

He went through his collection slowly and found that something prevented him from deleting any of his favourite indecent pictures. He had long ago convinced himself that he needed them when he had to clear his mind after an especially troubling trial.

However, right now he was tired. He'd come back to his task a bit later.

He locked his phone in the drawer of the nightstand near his bed and closed his eyes.

Sutton had been parked less than ten minutes when Constance Carroll drove out of the underground garage and rushed down the street. He followed her all the way to the hospital in the downtown area. He showed his badge to an attendant and was allowed to park in a reserved spot. Once inside the large building he followed the signs to the cardiac centre.

As he approached what he considered the hub of the centre, he saw Constance Carroll in conversation with a nurse. He waited until she left the area and followed at a distance until he saw which room she entered. He continued walking to the alcove at the end of the hallway where there were some chairs that looked comfortable. He sat in one of them, trying to decide his next move.

He realized that Mrs. Evers did not seem especially traumatized or nervous in any way because of her husband's condition. In fact, he had noticed that she walked with purpose, not slowly like a worried or frightened relative avoiding the inevitable as long as possible. But then again she was a murderer, so she had to be very much in control of her emotions at all times.

Sutton was certain that the woman would no doubt visit the judge for some time, so there was no reason for him to continue waiting at the end of the hallway. Especially since he had promised Anna that they could have a late lunch together. He made his way out of the hospital. As he drove back home he decided that a discussion with captain Corbett and with Walters the next morning would certainly result in an acceptable plan to catch the lady.

Constance Carroll Evers entered her husband's room and he opened his eyes. She smiled, pleased that he looked much better and that he was out of ICU. She kissed him.

"How are you feeling, dear?"

"There's still pain, of course," he said, "but I feel better."

"I was thinking that when you get out of here, we could go to the farm and really enjoy the rest of the spring and the summer."

He smiled. "Now, that's something to look forward to."

Discussing the Castle case the next day with Corbett and Walters, Sutton was fully aware that they didn't have any proof of wrongdoing on the part of the judge's wife. All they had was circumstantial evidence, something any lawyer worth his salt would destroy in a few minutes in a court of law. They had to widen their investigation.

The question was how to do it. Sutton felt he should continue to rely on his instincts to guide him as they reviewed the information they had collected so far, information which could perhaps let a new clue come into focus. That lull to review their findings was a somewhat slow quiet aspect of his work, one that required patience, but it was a quality he had mastered over the years.

Anna Sutton and her mother had finally taken the necessary steps to empty the room that little Bryan had enjoyed in his brief life. At times both women cried, but eventually the bed linens and all the clothes had been washed and neatly packed into boxes along with coats, shoes and boots. They had also packed all his toys and other accumulated things from the closet, even the window curtains.

"Since the pandemic, so many families are still having a hard time financially," Anna's mother said. "This is going to be so appreciated. A gift from a wonderful little boy," she said as she embraced her daughter one more time.

"Where are we going to take all this stuff?"

"I met a social worker when I was volunteering at the hospital. She told me about a group in this part of the city that distribute donations. I'm sure they'll be able to use all of it. Not too far from here."

"That's great."

Once the boxes were packed into Anna's vehicle, the two women went back into the room.

"You'll be keeping the furniture, I suppose," the older woman assumed.

"Yes. Josh and I are thinking of having another child."

"Just what the two of you need," her mother commented with a smile. "I'd love to be a grandmother again."

"You may very well have your wish."

The sun was shining once more for the two women.

CHAPTER FORTY-TWO

Dr. Brenda Castle shared office space with two other professionals. One was a podiatrist and the other a paediatrician, and the three shared the reception area and the bubbly Molly. She always met patients with a warm smile and oversaw all appointments so that things always ran efficiently.

Dr. Castle was at her desk finalizing notes for her last patient's file when Molly rang to tell her that her next appointment had arrived. That was her cue to go greet the woman in the reception area, something she always did with a new patient. Today it was especially important because a child was involved.

There seemed to always be children with a parent in the reception area waiting for the paediatrician so Castle had no idea who her new patient was. She called the name Liz Farmer and a casually dressed woman in her forties, who Castle thought looked tired, stood up. "That's me," she said as she got to her feet and approached the psychologist.

"I'd like to talk to you first before you see the child, but I can't leave her alone," Farmer said.

Before the psychologist could answer Molly quickly came to the rescue. "I can read to her. I do it for young patients all the time."

Liz Farmer looked at Castle. "Molly's great with kids. Your girl will be fine," she promised.

Farmer went to her charge, an angelic looking girl of six with beautiful curly blond hair. "Roma, the lady is going to read you a story, okay?" There was no answer but the girl stood and let herself be guided toward Molly who was taking out a few picture books from one of the drawers of her desk. The girl seemed intrigued, and Farmer was guided into the psychologist's office.

"Roma, what a lovely name," Brenda Castle commented as she went to sit behind her desk.

"Her mother told me she gave her daughter that name because she was conceived in Rome where they honeymooned," Farmer said as she took a chair in front of the desk.

"So, please tell me about Roma."

"Well, it's such a sad story. Her father was killed when the small plane in which he was a passenger crashed in a wooded area east of Toronto when Roma was just two years old. I got to know her mother, Allie, when she joined a group for grieving widows. I don't run the group, but I do attend from time to time to provide practical advice as needed. Allie was a lovely person, dedicated to Roma. She was a nurse and as such a front-line worker when the pandemic hit. As covid was winding down Allie caught the virus which she was unable to fight despite her young age. Such a tragedy. Roma went to live with her grandmother, Allie's mother, with whom she had already spent a lot of time while her mother was at work.

"I made a point of visiting occasionally just to see how the grandmother was coping as she grieved the death of her only child. I thought that things were going well until about a week and a half ago. That's when Roma stopped talking. I mean she doesn't say one word. She was in school, first grade, but the school told the grandmother that they couldn't cope with Roma and highly recommended professional help for the child. I tried talking with her, but there hasn't been any response. My GP recommended you so I thought you might be able to reach Roma.

"As you can imagine, the grandmother is beside herself. She doesn't understand what's happened to Roma, and she's on the waiting list for hip replacement surgery. She's asked me to find a temporary foster home for Roma while she recovers but it's impossible to place a child who doesn't talk. Have you ever had a similar case?"

"Not quite that sad I must say, but let me talk to her for a while and see where it goes."

"Great," Liz Farmer said as she stood. "Take your time. I have a book to keep me company."

The two women made their way to the reception area.

Molly had not only Roma's attention, but also that of two boys who were no doubt patients of the paediatrician. Molly who had been in that situation before quietly told the children that the doctor was ready now and that she would finish the story once the visit was over. The boys who were obviously twins quietly went back to their parents and the social worker formally introduced Roma to Brenda Castle who smiled, took the little girl's hand and led her into her office, closing the door.

"You can sit in that chair," Castle offered, as she pulled an elaborate chair fashioned to look like a throne closer to her desk. Roma sat in the unusual child's chair and the psychologist saw that the girl was fascinated by her seat.

"Do you like it?" Castle asked.

Roma nodded a yes.

"That chair was made for little girls who come to see me. You look like a little princess."

The girl almost smiled, and Castle saw that as a good sign.

"How old are you?"

Roma put one hand up along with one finger from the other.

"You're six."

The girl nodded again.

"Do you go to school?"

Again, a positive nod.

"Does your nana take you to school?"

This time the nod was negative.

Never mind, Castle thought, I'll get the information later. "Do you like going to school?"

The girl nodded forward again.

"Do you like your nana?"

Roma didn't move.

"Does she take you places?"

The girl nodded yes.

"That must be nice. Do you go to the park?"

Again a positive nod.

The psychologist saw there was pain in the large clear blue eyes that looked at her. "Did something happen in the park?"

Roma didn't move for a dozen seconds then slowly nodded. Yes.

"Did somebody hurt you?"

This time the positive nod was repeated a few times.

"A man hurt you?"

Again, yes.

"Did you know the man?"

The nod said no.

"Is that why you're mad at your grandma?"

Roma totally surprised Brenda Castle by saying: "Nana didn't stop him. She was talking to a lady."

"Well, maybe she didn't see the man. What did the man do? Did he touch you?"

"Yes. Behind a tree. I was scared. He lifted my dress."

"Did you scream?"

"Yes. Mommy told me I should scream when I was very scared."

"And then the man left?"

Roma nodded, and Brenda Castle was certain the worst was over for the beautiful and very sensitive child. She had expressed the difficult secret that she blamed her grandmother for the attack but couldn't tell her because she was the main person in her life now. Roma was mad at the nana she dearly loved, and by not talking it stayed a secret.

Brenda Castle stood and went to embrace the little girl who hugged her warmly in return.

"I want mommy," Roma said, and Brenda once again wondered why some people had such difficult roads to follow in this world.

CHAPTER FORTY-THREE

Dr. Castle released the little girl but kept holding her hand as she sat beside her.

"Your mommy is with the angels. She's happy and looking down at you. You can talk to her whenever you want."

"Nana told me but I want to see her."

"I know, sweetheart. I know, but you can look at her picture when you talk to her."

Roma had not thought of that and the idea pleased her. She smiled lightly. "Okay."

"Now, how would you like the lady in front to finish reading the story she was telling you?"

The girl nodded, obviously pleased. Dr. Castle opened the door for her and looked at her go to Molly who smiled and picked up the book.

Dr. Castle told Liz Farmer that she'd see her in a few minutes. She had a phone call to make.

Detective Josh Sutton answered his phone's ring. Brenda Castle identified herself.

"Dr. Castle, how are you?"

"As well as can be expected. Have you arrested my husband's killer yet?"

"Regrettably, no. We know who it is but we don't have enough evidence that would stand up in court. We are continuing to investigate."

"I'll feel safer when the person is in custody."

"Are you telling me that you think you and your family are in danger from the killer?"

"Not really, it's just that I'd feel better."

"I understand. We're doing our best."

"I'm sure you are. However, I'm calling on another matter. We discussed before that Murray had accessed a child porn site and that he was no doubt murdered because he wanted to help whoever the deranged man was. Well, I don't know if you're aware that there's a paedophile loose in a park in Toronto right now."

"We haven't been informed of any children being attacked."

"Well, detective, I can confirm that a sweet little girl of six was molested about a week and a half ago."

"How do you know that?"

"I just talked to her and she told me."

Sutton was lost for words for a moment, but rallied. "In what park did that happen?"

"I don't have that information right now, but I can easily get it. I'll get back to you shortly."

Sutton heard the line go dead and wondered about the good judge who was still in hospital. What was he doing a week and a half ago?

Dr. Castled called Liz Farmer back into her office. The social worker was smiling.

"You got her to talk?"

"I did. The reason she didn't talk was that she was holding on to a secret. She was molested in a park near her grandmother's home."

"Oh, no," Farmer exclaimed.

Castle explained her conversation with Roma and that she had contacted a police detective she knew. She said that he'd look into the assault, but he needed to know in what park it happened.

"I don't know," Farmer said, "but I'll ask the grandmother."

"May I suggest that you do it casually without revealing anything about the assault just now. It sounds like that woman has enough on her mind."

"Of course. I'll get back to you as soon as I can."

Josh Sutton heard back from Brenda Castle after Liz Farmer had talked to Roma's grandmother. The older woman had been thrilled that her young charge was finally talking, and when Liz asked her if she took Roma to a park, the older woman was proud to say that she did it as often as she could and identified the park in the neighbourhood.

When that last remark was related to the detective, it was clear to him that the judge may have been eyeing the little girl for days before he made his move. Since Roma and her grandmother went to the park right after an early dinner, around six or shortly after at this time of the year, Sutton wondered if the judge stopped at the park on the way home after work. A delay was always easy to explain because Toronto traffic could be a nightmare. The grandmother also said that they often went on Saturday and Sunday afternoon which must have tempted the judge to come up with an excuse to be away from his wife.

CHAPTER FORTY-FOUR

Sutton needed to have an overview of the judge's regular routine, so he and Walters made their way to the condo building where the Evers lived. Constance Carroll Evers was not especially pleased to see them arrive just as she was getting ready to go to the hospital to visit her husband.

"What is this intrusion all about?" she asked after the detectives had entered her unit.

"We would like to know your husband's usual routine," Sutton replied.

"What are you talking about? Why? Harry had heart surgery and is in hospital."

"That's why we came to you. We didn't want to disturb him."

"Why do you want to know his routine?" she asked.

"We have reason to believe that some superior court judges are being targeted by an individual, and we're hoping to establish a time-line. In the case of your husband, we want to make sure it did not cause his heart attack," Sutton explained.

The lawyer slowly sat down on the white sofa. "Are you sure?"

"At this point we can only suspect," Walters explained.

"What do you want to know?"

"Let's start with his weekday schedule. At what time did he get home usually?" Sutton asked.

"Always close to six thirty. That's his routine. Unless, of course, he's delayed because of traffic."

"I suppose that must happen often given that Toronto rush-hour traffic can be intense."

"It seems to be getting worse of late," she offered.

"I certainly agree with that," Sutton said. "What about weekends? Did he have responsibilities on Saturdays or Sundays?"

"Well, he did serve on a task force that looked at improving hiring policies regarding court personnel on Saturdays in the last few weeks. He said it was for only a month."

"Perhaps extra work contributed to his heart problem."

"I'm not sure. Difficult to assess."

"Well, that answers our questions. Now we'll get busy with the other judges. Thank you very much for your time."

"Happy to help," she said before closing the door behind the two detectives.

Later on her way to the hospital she would realize that the detectives had not offered any explanations about the cause of their concern for judges.

Traveling back to their division the detectives were certain that the lawyer had not seen through their yarn. At least, not yet

When Carroll stepped into her husband's room, she was pleased to see that some colour was back in his cheeks. He certainly looked better than in the previous days. She kissed him on the lips.

"How are you feeling, dear? You look a lot better."

"I do feel much better. I walk around without help now and should be able to go home in a couple of days."

"That's great. Some detectives came by the apartment a bit earlier asking about your routine. They said some judges were being targeted. Didn't say how, though. Know anything about that?"

"News to me," he told his wife, but he had a twinge of uneasiness. The kid in the park could have talked, but she didn't know who he was. His attempt at satisfying his demons had been a blunder from start to finish. He had been keeping an eye on the lovely girl for several days while planning every one of his movements. On the day he decided to attack he saw that the girl's grandmother was in deep conversation with another older woman and not paying attention to the girl who had gone with him when he asked her if the doll "over there" was hers.

When he had her pinned behind the tree, despite his threats, she screamed and at the same time a monstrous dog came at them barking his stupid head off, followed by the owner. He had no choice but to run away quickly. Now he wondered if the encounter had contributed to his heart attack. Probably not, he mused, because Doctor Joan had been urging him for some time to see a cardiologist which he had avoided.

"They said they had other judges to see, but somehow it didn't ring true."

"Why do you say that?"

"I've been a lawyer long enough to know when people are lying, or at least not telling the whole truth, and I'm sure these guys were hiding something." Just like you're doing now my darling, she thought. You're not listening to me because you know what it's all about.

"Well, no point in worrying about it. If it's anything, I'll hear about it."

Once his wife had left, despite his comforting words, the judge was seriously worried but wondered if the police were really investigating the attack in the park although he doubted they knew he was involved since the girl could not have identified him. He was sure of that. If they did suspect him for some reason, he couldn't do anything about it so he consoled himself by looking at the images of children on his phone.

The next morning, Constance Carroll got ready to go to her office for only the second time since her husband's health scare. Gabriel Mercer had offered to pick her up in his car because they were both involved in the same legal case and needed to stop to interview a witness, a mother with twin babies, who was too busy to go to their offices.

While waiting for Gabe Mercer in the well-appointed foyer of her building, Constance picked up a copy of the community newspaper that was delivered in their area every week and that the caretaker placed neatly on a table in the foyer. She liked to glance at it because there were always little tidbits of information concerning the neighbourhood that she found interesting. Also, the ads were all from local businesses and she made an effort to shop locally since the pandemic because so many local shops had been terribly affected while the virus raged as people turned to distance shopping online.

Today, she couldn't miss what looked like a last-minute addition to the copy of the front page with its screaming headline.

PAEDOPHILE ALERT.
Authorities are warning parents that a paedophile has been sighted in a west-end park. Police say he is usually seen in late afternoon, around dinner time. Everyone is urged to be on guard. (cont'd page 2)

Constance immediately got a bad feeling. The detectives had asked about the judge's routine because they suspected him of being the paedophile. That was clear to her now. She had not wanted to believe Murray Castle when he told her about the judge's child porn habit because she refused to see the love of her life for what he really was. At the time she saw Murray as expendable while her Harry was not.

But now things had changed. Her soul mate was no longer simply looking, he was doing. She could not be part of such sickness which would ruin them both. She had killed for him, to keep him, to protect their reputation. She now realized that it had been a colossal mistake and that Murray Castle was the better of the two men. He's the one who should have lived. After all, he had only wanted to help in contrast to Harry who was now trying to destroy the lives of precious children.

She was now facing herself squarely. When she married Harold, they had talked briefly about having children however he kept insisting that they should wait. They did just that while she tried to appease her desire to be a mother until it was too late for both of them. At that point she had suggested that they share their wealth by supporting summer camps for underprivileged children, and he had immediately agreed. Now she knew why. They had never visited the camps because she was certain that doing so would play havoc with her psyche. Would Harold have visited the camps without her? No. She always knew where he was, at least she consoled herself that she did most of the time.

What a mess! How could she have so misjudged the only man in her life, the one she had always supported as he rose to the bench, the one she had loved for so many years? How could she not have seen the demon that drove him to such immorality?

She was trying to determine what her next step should be when

Mercer's car came to a stop in front of her building. When she got in, he apologized for being late, but she dismissed his remark as unnecessary.

CHAPTER FORTY-FIVE

It was almost four o'clock when Constance Evers finished putting her files away neatly after instructing her paralegal and her assistant about the most important issues on her calendar.

She told them she had just gotten a call from the hospital informing her that the judge had taken a turn for the worse, so she had to rush out and might have to be away for several days. They were to inform Gabriel Mercer of any legal issued that came up. She took time to stop by Gabriel Mercer's office to tell him the same thing. He wished her and Harold well.

Harold Evers was surprised, but obviously happy to see his wife come in before his dinner had been served. He was sitting in a comfortable chair looking at his phone, but immediately turned it off. She thought he looked well but could hardly control the deep sadness caught at the bottom of her soul since her decision. She had faced reality and decided on the only road she could follow.

"Hi, Connie. Everything okay?"

"Sure. I just left the office a little early so we could spend time together."

"I like that."

She bent down and kissed him on the lips for longer than he had anticipated.

"I really like that."

Boy, this was difficult! Perhaps she should wait? No, her decision had been made after hours of personal deliberation and the knowledge that there was no other avenue she could pursue. She couldn't let her husband be paraded in front of her colleagues, in front of her clients, in front of the Toronto judiciary, in front of the world for what he really was. Fortunately, a dead person cannot be charged. And a hospital is where people die, especially those who have had serious health issues.

She reached into her expensive handbag and retrieved a small plastic bottle. "I got you some vitamin C to shore up your immune system. I'm sure your doctor would approve."

"Of course. Thanks."

She uncapped the bottle and took out a round pink tablet. "Do you want to take it now?" she asked.

"Why not? I read somewhere that taking vitamins before a meal is always good."

"You're right," she said looking at her watch. "Listen I've got to make a call. I'll leave the pill here on your table with your water. Take it whenever you want. I won't be long."

She stepped out into the corridor, closing the door behind her and holding her breath for a moment. Killing Murray Castle had been easy enough because she had been propelled by rage at his perceived impertinence. While he was in discussion with other lawyers in the conference room, she had quickly reached for the vitamin container in his jacket pocket and added the aconite tablet to it. It had been a breeze.

A while later she had walked by the door to Castle's office just at the moment he put the pill in his mouth. She had hurried on, pleased to see it happen rather than wondering when he would decide to ease his allergy symptoms. Screaming by Castle's son had followed and a doctor was called. Surely the doctor could not suspect poison. How could he? But he had, and now the police was circling. But they would never be able to prove anything, no matter how hard detective Sutton tried, because there was no proof. It had been a simple, quiet, perfect murder that had made her feel in control.

Killing her Harry was a totally different matter. She knew that she didn't have the courage to see him take the pill and convulse until he died to have that image remain in front of her eyes the rest of her life.

Yet, of course, even if she wouldn't actually see it happening, she was certain she would nevertheless picture it in her mind and would always regret it, but there was no other way.

She walked quickly down to the end of the corridor not turning around when medical personnel rushed into her husband's room because his heart monitor had alerted them that something was amiss. She got into one of the elevators and made her way down to the cafeteria just as detective Sutton got off the next elevator.

He stepped into Evers' room while the medical personnel were fussing over the judge and attempting to revive him. Sutton was still standing just inside the room when a rather slim man with a stethoscope around his neck pronounced Harold Evers dead at five-oh-six. Sutton did not miss the strong smell of the vomit near the chair where the judge was still sitting.

Sutton approached, showed his badge, and asked for the physician in charge of Evers' file. The slender man with the stethoscope replied that he was the one on duty.

Sutton then told him that he had reasons to believe that Evers' wife might have wanted to kill him. He added that he wanted the body to be examined immediately for any traces of aconite.

"Aconite? Are you sure? Odd poison," the doctor commented.

"Believe me I know what I'm talking about."

"Very well. I'll talk to his surgeon and we'll proceed from there."

"His wife must be kept in the dark," Sutton emphasized.

"What do you want us to do?"

The detective elaborated a plan for the medical personnel and in a moment, orderlies were taking the lifeless body of judge Harold Evers away.

Twenty minutes later Mrs. Evers walked back into her husband's room only to find it empty. She rushed to the nurses' station and was told that he was in surgery. "But why? He was doing well."

"You need to ask the doctor. All we can tell you is that he's being well taken care of. It's certainly going to take a while. Why don't you go home and rest."

She nodded absentmindedly at the middle-aged nurse and went to sit in one of chairs in the alcove at the end of the hallway. She was in shock. Certainly not because Harold was in distress, but because his survival had not even entered her mind. The pill had killed Murray Castle quickly. What was happening here? Perhaps that type of pill quickly loss potency. Perhaps she should have stored it differently. Perhaps in the freezer. She was a lawyer, not a damn toxicologist! What a terrible mistake on her part to believe that she had all the answers.

But what if Harry had not taken the pill? She had simply left it on his table after all. She had not seen him swallow it. The medical emergency might simply be the result of some cardiac issue. She had to relax and wait to see what happened next. Or she could be proactive in order to ease her mind.

She stood and rushed into her husband's room. There was only a glass of water on the table but it didn't telegraph any confirmation that the judge had taken the poisoned pill although there was vomit on the floor. She immediately remembered that that was one of the effects of the poison, but he had survived since he was now in surgery.

She stood unmoving for a moment wondering how her plan had gone so awry. If she had waited for him to take the pill she would know exactly what was going on. Now she could only speculate that he might have vomited the poison and that he was simply be facing another heart problem. What a nightmare, she thought, feeling suddenly very old and tired.

She had to go home and stop chastising herself.

CHAPTER FORTY-SIX

As soon as she closed the door to her condo unit she went into the kitchen, opened the door to the well stocked wine cabinet and took out a bottle of red wine without looking at the label. In a moment she was pouring herself a healthy measure into a large glass.

As she sipped on the sofa in the living room she was contemplating that when she asked, and paid, Joe Blanchard to provide poisoned pills she had requested three off the top of her head without really thinking it through. She had only planned to kill Murray, so one pill was enough, but she had told him that three would be needed for her non-existing case because she always liked to be prepared. What if something happened and she needed more than one?

And when she decided that her husband had to go, having two extra pills made the decision to stop the miserable paedophile in his track so much easier.

But what if the cardiac surgeon detected the aconite if her husband had not vomited all of it? She was used to expect all unexpected possibilities before arguing a case in court, which had not been the case here. Killing the man in her life, the man she had always loved, and still did, despite everything, was a whole different ball game that stabbed at her whole emotional reserve.

As she continued to sip wine, ever more urgently, she realized that her internal passion leading to the decision to murder Harold had been too intense to foresee all possible details. She had been guided by shame and fear.

A huge mistake.

Having slept only a couple of hours the night before while she examined all aspects of her new reality, she was now totally exhausted given her quick intake of wine. She carefully placed her empty glass on the coffee table and stretched her body on the white sofa. In a moment she was snoring quietly, dead to the world.

The constant annoying sound of a buzzer had become part of Constance's dream where a judge was banging his gavel to call order in the courtroom. When it didn't stop she woke up suddenly. It took her several seconds to shake the cobwebs from her brain and realize that it was the door buzzer that was calling her to attention.

She sat up on the side of the sofa and looked at her watch which indicated ten o'clock. She went to the kitchen and splashed cold water on her face in an effort to wake up as the buzzer continued to annoy her. Who the hell could it be? Then she realized that someone could be coming to tell her that her dear husband had not survived the surgery.

She went to the wall-mounted mirror near the front door and made an effort to comb her hair with her fingers without much success, then pressed the button to see and hear who was so rudely disturbing her sleep. She recognized detective Sutton.

"What's so urgent."

"I'm detective Sutton."

I know who you are, buddy. I can see you and part of your partner standing in front of the camera.

"We need to talk to you, Mrs. Carroll."

"Does it have to be now? I was asleep."

"It can't wait."

She buzzed the door's unlocking devise. As the door unlatched, detectives Sutton and Walters entered, followed by two uniformed policemen. They made their way to the elevators.

As they rode up to the tenth floor Sutton could certainly find satisfaction in having finally come to realize that the judge might be in danger from his murderess wife while he was in the hospital. The detective who, when working a case was always analyzing and reviewing, had come to the conclusion that the lady might have ordered more than one pill. Who knew when another murder might solve a problem? And Harold Evers was certainly a problem for her now because she had certainly deduced that he was considered the prime suspect for the attack on little Roma in the park.

His fears were confirmed when he returned to the hospital after having dinner with Anna. The medical examiner had proof that the judge had been poisoned with aconite. They could now arrest his wife without fear that the case was not solid. Sutton contacted Walters, and they made their plan to arrest the lady in her condo that evening which was the reason uniformed officers were along.

By the time Josh Sutton pressed the bell to her unit, Constance had managed to comb her hair and change from a wrinkled blouse to a casual cotton top. She opened the door and invited the detectives in with a sweep of her hand. Both men stepped inside, while Sutton made sure that the door would remain ajar.

Sutton went immediately to the problem at hand. "Mrs. Carroll, you are under arrest for the murder of your husband Harold Evers and the murder of Murray Castle."

"What are you talking about," she nearly yelled. "My husband is probably still in surgery..."

"No. He's not. He's in the morgue. An autopsy has confirmed that he was poisoned with aconite." Sutton emphasized.

She starred at the detective. How could her decision end up in such a way!

"Please come with us," Walters was now saying.

She nodded. "I need to call a lawyer before I go anywhere with you."

"You can call your lawyer at the division," Sutton said.

"No. I want to do it now," she said loudly and walked into her bedroom, closing the door behind her.

Sutton signalled to the uniformed officers to step inside as they waited.

She had envisaged everything, or so she thought. Her possible arrest had not been truly considered. It had always been glossed over in her mind as a step would never come into focus. Now it was a reality from which she could not escape. It had come about because she had let her emotions get in the way, but killing the one person in the world you truly love was not an easy task, she mused. Now there was no way to forgive herself. Because of her mistakes she would now spend the rest of her life in prison and be the totally unwelcome felony-poster-lawyer of the Toronto legal community. What a mess!

She could not let that happen.

She opened the top drawer of her bureau and her hand searched for the little plastic bag hidden underneath a pile of silk scarves. She looked at it for only a second because she didn't want to lose her nerve, then took out the remaining pink pill and slipped it into her mouth. She swallowed quickly and after just a few moments pain was quickly excruciating in her stomach as she let her body fall to the floor all the while screaming in agony.

On hearing the noise, Sutton quickly ran to open the bedroom door. Seeing her efforts to breathe he knew instantly that she had swallowed an aconite tablet. She was choking as her body attempted to vomit an empty stomach. He yelled to Walters to call an ambulance, but in just a few moments, as her body abruptly shut down, she stopped moving.

While the coroner and the forensics team were conducting their examination Sutton had asked for an autopsy. After the body had been removed the two detectives and the two officers made their way back to their division for a debriefing with captain Corbett. It had all ended sadly and the judge and his wife would never face charges.

Sutton was mentally examining the possibility that extra pills had been ordered by the lawyer to satisfy a "should-it-come-to-that plan" in case. In fact it could very well have been insurance so that cherished reputations were not sullied.

CHAPTER FORTY-SEVEN

Before it got too late, Sutton called Dr. Brenda Castle. She picked up after one ring.

"Detective. It's late. I assume it's important."

"It definitely is. We know who killed your husband and we thought you'd want to know as soon as possible even if it can only be on the phone given the late hour."

"Yes, of course. Very considerate of you."

As he once again detailed the Murray Castle case, she listened hardly believing what she heard.

"You mean to tell me that Murray was murdered for the simple reason that he was hoping to steer the judge to get help? This confirms my theory that the world is on a downward spiral because people refuse to face mental disorders head on. I mean depression and anxiety problems have exploded since the pandemic yet many people don't think it's important. The judge had a personality disorder that was deeply disturbing, but rather than seek psychological help he held on to his secret, not even discussing it with his wife. But she had figured it out and decided to cover up this serious issue rather than helping him. No doubt the aim being what I call keeping up appearances, in this case their reputation.

"A large segment of society still sees a mental problem as shameful when it's only one of the many hurdles we humans all encounter in this life. It's all very sad. I take it that judge Evers was the one who attacked little Roma in the park?"

"We believe so, yes."

"Thank you for letting me know about Murray, detective. It doesn't make me feel better but it's one step toward closure."

"Hopefully it will be soon. On another matter, while I have you on the phone, Dr. Castle, I feel you should know that the RCMP will be arresting someone you know on charges of visiting child porn sites, Norbert Perkins."

"Garrett's father?"

"Yes. It's something we came across during the investigation of the death of your husband. It looks like Garrett is not the only one in the family with mental problems."

"Indeed. I appreciate knowing."

His next call was to Gabriel Mercer at home. Sutton had seen the importance of entering the numbers of the case's go-to-man in his phone should they be needed. The lawyer answered in a questioning voice when he saw that the call was coming from the police.

"Detective Sutton, Mr. Mercer. Sorry to call so late but this couldn't wait."

"I have a feeling that this isn't good news."

"Quite right, sir."

Sutton spent some time explaining how the Murray Castle murder case had evolved and how it had all ended. He detailed the steps leading to the charges that had been waiting for judge Evers, but most of all the ones they had against his wife.

Mercer was silent so long that Sutton asked: "Sir, are you okay?"

"Sorry. I'm fine. I just can't believe all this was the result of Murray wanting to help the judge. And Connie, how can I have misjudged her so much. Incredible. You are sure that she committed suicide?"

"An autopsy is on the way to confirm, but I saw her die and I can assure you that she ingested a poisonous substance."

"I simply don't understand," Mercer stated.

"I will confirm the cause of death as soon as we have the official result of the autopsy."

"Thank you. I appreciate that."

"Humans are complicated, especially murderers," Sutton offered, adding: "On another matter we don't have information about relatives of the Evers, so we could not advise anyone of the deaths."

"I'll take care of that. Thank you, detective, for all your work. You know, I thought that once I knew who had killed Murray that I'd feel better. I really don't."

"I certainly appreciate that," Sutton offered.

There was nothing else to add, so the detective told the lawyer that he should call if he needed more details.

It was well past one o'clock by the time Sutton got home after promising his captain that he would write a detailed report the next morning. Tonight, he was too disappointed. He had not at any time during the investigation contemplated that a second murder and a suicide were possibilities. But, he consoled himself, it was almost impossible to foresee why some people can react to their secrets, their frustrations and their narrow view of events by deciding to commit murder. It was a reality that would always be part of his work.

Anna had been asleep, but she heard him and joined him in the kitchen as he drank from a bottle of beer.

"Sorry, honey. I didn't mean to wake you."

"No problem. Everything okay?"

"Just a hell of night," he replied, sitting at the kitchen table.

She sat near him, but remained quiet.

"I just want to relax for a bit, get the day out of my head."

She stood and went to put her arms around him. The gesture of love was a starting point for reducing his disappointment at how the Castle case had finally ended.

CHAPTER FORTY-EIGHT

A day later, when Josh Sutton went back into his office after interviewing a witness in a robbery case, Ross Walters came to sit across from his desk.

"Here's the latest. London has scratched Henry Fisher from its lists of Canadians caught on child porn sites. The rest of the names were sent to the RCMP, and Norbert Perkins was taken into custody last evening at his home. He appeared in court this morning where his lawyer argued that he didn't belong in custody because he suffered from a mental disorder called voyeurism. He's been granted bail."

"Not a bad defence I suppose. We'll let the court figure it out," Sutton said. "You know, Dr. Castle is no doubt right when she says that people don't pay enough attention to mental illness. Then again, sufferers seem very adept at hiding whatever disorder or issue guides their lives like we saw with paedophilia where secrecy is of the utmost importance. One of the reasons, of course, being that it's illegal."

"The Castle case certainly took us on a road I never expected," Walters said. "But at least we got some very sick people to stop abusing children."

"Amen to that, although we have no idea how men become paedophiles, do we?"

"Unfortunately no, but in time ..."

"You know, Ross, I admire the fact that you're always positive.

You've been a good influence on me in my darkest hours. I appreciate it."

"All in a day's work," Walters commented with a smile.

On Friday when Dr. Joe Blanchard went to pick up his son, his ex-wife surprised him by asking if he could take their son until Monday morning. He saw that she was distraught.

"What's going on, Susan? Did something happen?"

"Didn't you hear on the news? Auntie Connie and uncle Harold are both dead."

"What? What happened? An accident?"

"No. The police say Connie killed herself by ingesting some poison."

"I can't believe that," Joe said although he could not deny knowing exactly what type of poison she had taken.

"They also say that she killed uncle Harold."

"You can't be serious. It makes no sense. Whenever I saw them they always seemed to love each other so much. They were always so very attentive to each other. "

"I know. My family's going to ask for more details and proofs. In the meantime I'm going to be busy with my relatives all weekend. There's the question of the wills, then trying to decide what to do with their condo, the furniture and all the rest. So, is it okay? Can you take your son to school on Monday?"

"Of course. No problem. My sympathies, Susan."

"Thanks."

While driving toward his condo, Blanchard was distracted. He was only now fully realizing that Connie had had a plan all along. From the aconite tablets he had made, he gave—rather sold--three to Connie because he had fallen for her con. He was convinced that she knew exactly what she was doing, and he should have asked more questions, be more of a man instead of a gambler out of control drooling at the thought of more money to gamble away. But, he had to admit that he frankly never in his wildest dreams thought that his ex-wife's aunt would go on a killing spree. Women simply didn't do such things!

No matter his quarrel with his ex-wife he knew that she was a nurturing creature. He had seen it ever since their son had been born, and he was convinced that all women were as protecting of life as she was. There was no way she would consider murder. Yet, her aunt Connie had gone completely off the track. He wondered why.

He concluded that the only reason was that something in her brain went awry.

"Dad, can we go on a hot air balloon on Sunday?"

"Why not?" Blanchard answered. "If the weather stays nice."

"It will," the boy said with a wide smile.

Time to leave murder and suicide behind and enjoy life, Joe Blanchard thought. At least Connie was now giving him more time with his son. A welcomed silver lining resulting from a sea of stupidity.

Liz Farmer was still working to find a good home for little Roma, but it was not easy since it was to be only for a few months. The social worker was convinced that the little girl needed to be placed in a home where she was the centre of attention for a while to counteract the many losses in her life. The foster families Farmer knew looked after more than one child because they thought it was best for the youngsters. But here the needs were different. Farmer had to look elsewhere, perhaps find a young couple who could not get pregnant.

Then she thought of her volunteer friend and her daughter Anna who was still mourning the loss of a son. That could very well be a good avenue for a single temporary placement. She called her friend.

Anna and her mother met with Liz Farmer at her office. The social worker explained the situation in which little Roma found herself. Anna listened attentively. Farmer finally asked how would she feel about taking care of the little girl until her grandmother had fully recovered from her surgery?

"You've both lost someone you love, it could help both of you," Liz Farmer offered. "And Roma is an intelligent, darling girl."

"I certainly had not thought about taking care of a child, but it could be fun. I have to discuss it with my husband before making a decision.

"Of course. Of course."

"I take it you must have looked into our backgrounds," Anna said. "So I assume that the fact that I spent time in a mental hospital is not a problem."

Liz Farmer had not, in fact, examined the Suttons as she would normally have done with other prospective foster parents. Here there was urgency and Anna's mother had only praise for her daughter and her detective son-in-law who faced and survived the tragedy of their young son.

Playing the role of a professional who had crossed all her t's, Farmer commented the obvious: "The time spent in hospital served you well, did it not?"

"Yes. I was finally able to accept that Bryan was dead which I was not ready to do before I went to Montrose. My therapist, Dr. Maxwell, helped me to face my hurt squarely."

While Liz Farmer was fully aware that young Roma didn't need any more drama in her young life, she could feel that Anna was now ready to go forward, emotionally enriched by having finally faced and accepted her loss.

Josh Sutton was once again driving the northern section of Marshall road during his midday break. The beautiful August weather was making him smile, but that was not the only reason. Anna was where she belonged, always smiling as she continued to mother the lovely Roma, teaching her new skills, playing with her while waiting for her grandmother to be fully recovered. His wife had dared venture into a new life where she finally recognized that Bryan would never leave because he would always be a bright guiding light for both of them.

These days Josh saw no need to scream at the virus as he had done every day over a long period of time. The pandemic was gone and a new road was clear. It was time to leave the sorrow behind and turn to the future. Of course, the funny thing about the future, he mused, is that you never know what it's going to be like. But whatever was ahead, he would be able to face it because he had lived through despair and was now very much aware of the truth in the old adage that what does not kill a man makes him better.

The future could only be more indulgent now that they had confirmation that Anna was pregnant and that they would welcome a child in the spring. It would be a complete renewal.

He prayed the Universe would smile on them and send them as lovely a little girl as Roma.

ABOUT THE AUTHOR

D.B. Crawford writes in a variety of genres. Her psychology background serves her well in creating fictitious characters. She lives in Montreal.